KV-635-946

992287221 8

SPECIAL MESSAGE TO READERS

This book is published under the auspices of

THE ULVERSCROFT FOUNDATION

(registered charity No. 264873 UK)

Established in 1972 to provide funds for research, diagnosis and treatment of eye diseases. Examples of contributions made are: —

A new Children's Assessment Unit at Moorfield's Hospital, London.

•

Twin operating theatres at the Western Ophthalmic Hospital, London.

•

A Chair of Ophthalmology at the University of Leicester.

•

The establishment of a Royal Australian College of Ophthalmologists "Fellowship".

You can help further the work of the Foundation by making a donation or leaving a legacy. Every contribution, no matter how small, is received with gratitude. Please write for details to:

THE ULVERSCROFT FOUNDATION,
The Green, Bradgate Road, Anstey,
Leicester LE7 7FU, England.
Telephone: (0116) 236 4325

In Australia write to:

THE ULVERSCROFT FOUNDATION,
c/o The Royal Australian College of Ophthalmologists,
27, Commonwealth Street, Sydney,
N.S.W. 2010.

LOVE ON TURTLE ISLAND

When television researcher Jenna Fervair arrives in Costa Rica to investigate the work of naturalist Professor Kim Oates, she discovers that the professor is not the middle-aged spinster that she had anticipated, but a ruggedly handsome young man. Soon she finds herself sharing many exciting adventures with him, and a relationship develops between them. Beset by difficulties, Jenna and Kim independently strive to cross the abyss of distance and lifestyle that separates them.

THERESA MURPHY

LOVE ON TURTLE ISLAND

Complete and Unabridged

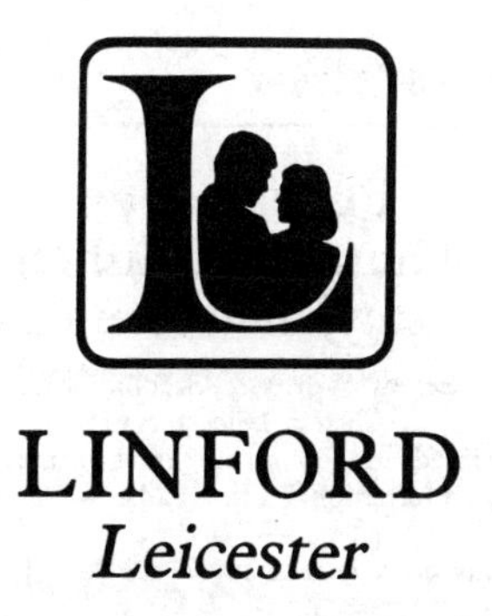

LINFORD
Leicester

First published in Great Britain in 1992 by
Robert Hale Limited

British Library CIP Data

Murphy, Theresa, *1962–*
Love on Turtle Island.—Large print ed.—
Linford romance library
1. Love stories
2. Large type books
I. Title
823.9′14 [F]

ISBN 0–7089–5236–4

Published by
F. A. Thorpe (Publishing) Ltd.
Anstey, Leicestershire

Set by Words & Graphics Ltd.
Anstey, Leicestershire
Printed and bound in Great Britain by
T. J. International Ltd., Padstow, Cornwall

This book is printed on acid-free paper

1

THE taxi-driver indicated before steering the cab off the motorway, slowing down the vehicle on the slip road on the approach to Heathrow. It was early morning. The journey out from London hadn't taken long; the normally traffic-cluttered and busy motorway was quiet at breakfast-time.

But now the road leading to the airport was blocked by a massive traffic jam, with dozens of cars, coaches and commercial vehicles stretching in long lines in the lanes ahead of the cab. The time saved on the journey out from the capital would be wasted now.

"They're 'aving a security practice 'ere this mornin'," the cockney driver explained, half turning in his seat to speak to his passenger, Jenna Fervair, who sat in the rear of the taxi. "We're goin' to be in this queue for some time.

There ain't no way around it. What time does your flight leave?"

"Not for another hour and a half."

Jenna always erred on the side of caution, arriving long before the time of her departure, knowing the lengthy hold-ups that could happen unexpectedly at an airport.

"Goin' far, are you?" The taxi-driver, in an effort to pass the time pleasantly, tried to make small talk.

"Costa Rica."

"Phew! That's some way!" He whistled through his teeth. "On business, are you?"

The smart, costumed appearance of Jenna, combined with her neatly trimmed dark, shoulder-length hair gave her away as a professional person. She carried an air of maturity in excess of her twenty-three years.

"Yes. I am."

The conversation ceased as the cars in front began to move, covering only a short distance before stopping, then moving off again, before coming to a halt. This allowed Jenna the opportunity to re-read the letter from Professor Oates that had arrived at her Covent Garden office the previous day. Kim Oates was her contact in Costa Rica, and also the reason why Jenna was flying out.

Jenna worked as a researcher for one of the many independent film companies that had formed after the de-regularization of the British television network. Concentrating on documentaries, mainly natural history, the company was so intrigued to hear the story of British-born Professor Oates' study of animals and birds native to Costa Rica, that they made plans to document the professor's work.

It was Jenna who would be doing the film producer's groundwork, finding out all the information she could and reporting back. It would be according to the strength of her research that a decision would be made whether to go ahead with the project.

" . . . I look forward to meeting you

at the airport . . . "

Kim ended this letter, like all previous correspondence, on a friendly note.

According to an earlier letter, Kim had graduated from Bristol University, which gave them something in common, as Jenna had been born, and grew up in that city before, when she was twelve years old, her family — parents and two older brothers — had moved to London, where her French-born father had secured the post of editor on a major national weekly newspaper.

Jenna had been working for A.Z.T. Associates for nearly two years, loving every minute of the interesting and varied work. She felt sorry for those in her peer group who flitted from job to job, unable to settle to anything and uncertain as to their future plans. Jenna had chosen the film industry for a career in her early teens, and was delighted to have achieved her goal so early on in her working life.

Jenna finished reading the letter and

returned it to its envelope. It was only just March, yet Jenna had already been abroad twice since the beginning of the year. Her job had made her something of a globe-trotter. In early January she had spent a fortnight in Spain interviewing pro- and anti-bullfighting campaigners, and in mid-February her work had taken her to the eastern coast of America for a whistle-stop three days, where she attempted, but failed, to track down the origin of a rumour that a type of wild cat, thought to be extinct, had been spotted in the forests of Connecticut: a story that eventually was proved to be a hoax.

"Keep the change," Jenna called back to the taxi-driver, as she hurriedly left the cab, after handing him a twenty-pound note when they at last reached the airport.

They had taken longer than she had anticipated to cover the distance over which the queue had stretched, consequently making it necessary for her to rush to catch her flight. Carrying only one small suitcase, she was able to run easily — checking in with just minutes to spare.

Once the preliminary safety precautions had been dealt with and the aeroplane took off, Jenna checked out the in-flight movie, which turned out to be the same comedy she had seen only weeks before on her return flight from the States, then settled down in her window seat to read a magazine and catch up on some badly needed sleep.

* * *

Jenna pulled her sunglasses down from the top of her head to shade out the brilliant burning ball of fire that glared down on her as she disembarked from the aircraft at San José airport. The air was thick with a sticky heat; perspiration ran from Jenna's brow. It was in stark contrast to the chilly winter climate she had left in London.

Her big blue eyes scanned the crowd awaiting arrivals as she walked down the aeroplane steps, searching for the professor. But what did Kim Oates look like? She had no idea.

A woman who fitted her mental image of Kim was standing to the side of the crowd. In her mid-forties, the woman's greying hair was drawn back into a bun. That must be her, Jenna decided; she had the smart, but still slightly eccentric look of a professor — a preconception Jenna had of well-educated people, indoctrinated as she was by countless movies and books. The woman waved. Just as Jenna was about to raise her hand, a couple who had sat in the seats immediately in front of her on the aircraft, returned the woman's greeting.

Kim Oates hadn't put in an appearance by the time Jenna made her way through the time-consuming officialdom of the airport and out to the taxi rank in front of the main terminal building. Possibly they had missed each other, through Professor Oates being delayed, so Jenna planned to take a cab to the address on the professor's letter, somewhere in a place called Tamarindo, which could have been any distance from the airport — Jenna hadn't the foggiest notion.

A klaxon horn drew her attention sharply to an ageing grey-coloured American estate car that came speeding into the airport's precincts and toward the taxi rank. The whole car was a scrap heap on wheels, seemingly held together by rust. It rattled and creaked as it drew up alongside Jenna.

If this is the general standard of taxi, I'll walk, Jenna thought to herself, as she stepped back from the kerb. The car was a left-hand drive model with the driver sitting on the opposite side of the car to which Jenna was standing.

"I no want *carro d'alquiler*." In her broken and halting Spanish, the chief language of Costa Rica, Jenna told the driver she didn't want a cab.

The man, hidden by shadows, sitting behind the steering-wheel leant across the car to open the passenger door.

He is being persistent, Jenna thought, moving away from the car.

"Miss Fervair?" he called.

"Yes?" Jenna turned back.

"I'm Kim Oates. Sorry not to have been here when your flight landed." A large, sun-tanned hand, with long artistic fingers reached out to shake hers. "Throw your case in the back and we'll be on our way."

Jenna pulled on the handle of the rear door of the car, but it was jammed closed.

"Best to toss it over the seat," Professor Oates advised. "The rear doors are stuck."

Jenna did as he suggested, and got into the car, finding the interior no more presentable than the exterior. She was slowly recovering from her surprise at discovering Kim Oates was a man, and adjusting to the fact that he wasn't the middle-aged spinster she had been expecting to meet.

Seeing him clearly for the first time, he proved to be a very handsome man if only he removed the floppy panama-type hat and mirrored sunglasses.

"Welcome to Costa Rica," he greeted her as he sped the car away from the airport, at motorway speed in an urban area.

"I wasn't expecting . . . er," Jenna stumbled over her words.

"You weren't expecting a chap," he laughed, filling in for her while at the same time putting her at her ease.

"No, I wasn't," she confessed, blushing slightly.

"Don't worry, you aren't the first. It's a common mistake. My parents named me after Rudyard Kipling's fictional Kim. They both loved the book. Though it's a unisex name, most people normally associate it with a female," he told her as they drove down the narrow crowded San José streets, people, animals and motor vehicles sharing the roads, with his and his fellow drivers' method of navigating the packed thoroughfares being the constant blaring of the car's horn and a foot flat down on the accelerator. "Now I only use Kim for my work. People call me by my middle name of Greg."

It suits you much better than Kim, Jenna thought. It was a more rugged name that fitted this lean and muscular man ideally.

Jenna stretched her legs out in the car's footwell in an attempt at easing the cramp caused by the long flight. She grimaced with pain.

"Forgive me. I should have asked how you are," Greg noticed her distress. "My manners aren't too good."

"I'm just slightly tired after the flight, nothing too serious."

"Good." Greg steered the car violently round an old and rickety oxcart that was travelling slowly in the centre of the street. "As you can see, we have few traffic regulations. At least, ones we obey."

Jenna had noticed. The driving in San José was more in keeping with dodgem cars at the fairground than a city street. She could also understand why the car was so battered, as there appeared to be accidents on nearly every street corner, involving every type of transport. Each incident was followed by a great deal of hot tempered Hispanic arguing.

"I've organized a room for you in my home in Tamarindo. My house is right on the Pacific Coast, in a beautiful spot. I thought you would prefer that to staying in one of the hotels reserved for *turistas*."

"Thank you. When possible I prefer not to stay in a tourist hotel."

Greg had to slow the car as they became involved in a traffic jam caused by a horse-drawn cart shedding its load. Soon they were round the obstruction.

"We have a journey of some hours ahead of us. Would you care to eat?"

"I'd love to. I am hungry. On the flight I only had a light snack. I find heavy meals extenuate my jet-lag."

"There's a café just out of the city

where they make a wonderful *gallo pinto*."

"*Gallo pinto*? What's that? The name sounds intriguing."

"It's rice, peppers, black beans and onions mixed together. Normally I have it for breakfast. A custom I picked up from the *Ticos*. It's absolutely delicious, I guarantee you'll want seconds."

He continued driving, several times causing Jenna's heart to leap to her mouth, as they narrowly avoided a collision with other road-users, be it an animal or motor vehicle.

As the sun streamed in through the car's windscreen such a heat built up in the vehicle, that even opening all the windows didn't get rid of it. Jenna loosened the collar of her blouse, trying to cool down.

"It is hot," agreed Greg, taking his hat off to fan himself with it. "During the day the temperature is somewhere between seventy and eighty degrees. Obviously it's hotter in a car. At night it dips down to sixty degrees, or so."

Before he had removed his hat, Jenna suspected his hair was receding, and vanity had him keep it covered. Nothing could have been further from the truth. As he took off his headgear a shock of black curly hair was revealed. The glossy waves tumbled down over his head, in places touching his denim shirt-collar. Without the hat he looked much younger than what Jenna had assessed to be his thirty years.

"Do you ever get used to the heat?"

"Never. I've been here six years and I still don't feel comfortable in it." He suddenly changed the subject. "Look over there. That's Costa Rica's National Museum, majestic place, isn't it?"

For the next few miles Greg acted more like a tourist guide than a professor, pointing out to her the National Theatre and the National Art Museum, frequently taking one or both hands off the steering-wheel to explain something about the places to her. It was obvious he deeply loved the country where he had made his home.

As the buildings became fewer and open spaces more frequent, the heat noticeably decreased, though Jenna still felt like she was trapped in a greenhouse.

"You'll see some lovely scenery on the trip down to Tamarindo," Greg told her, as she marvelled at her scenic surroundings. "We have to travel through the National Park Manuel Antonio. Despite the term 'park', you'll find it's nothing like an English park. It consists of mainly a dense, wet jungle. It's like a genuine safari park. You'll see all types of wildlife, monkeys, iguanas and lots more, though it may be too dark to see much. We have the small city of Quepos to go through before that. They are not too far apart, both are in the Puntarenas province. First, let's eat."

As he spoke Greg braked the car sharply, swinging it off the road into a dusty parking lot in front of a small shack which a sign, suspended above, claimed to be a café. Leaving the car amid huge trucks and lorries, Jenna was reminded by the place of a typical English greasy-spoon transport café, full of cigarette smoke and jukebox noise.

Greg met her at the front of the car. He towered above her, and subconsciously bent over to speak to her. He must have been at least six feet tall, a full ten inches taller than her. His sunglasses reflected her image, with her strong yet petite features, pencil-thin pink lips, big blue eyes and narrow nose, a winning combination that had brought her many admirers.

Greg looked more like a beach bum than an intellectual professor. His tanned legs were bare from his trainers up to his cut-off denims.

The café was so crowded that they sat at a table outside the shack as if it were a Parisian street coffee house. Eating *al fresco* was preferable to the airless, suffocating heat of the shack's interior.

Greg ordered their food at a counter in the café, returning to sit across the table from Jenna. He had taken off his sunglasses and hung them from the pocket of his shirt.

For the first time, Jenna saw his face bare of adornment. He had dark, almost Latin-type features, deep brown eyes the focal point of his face, as if they reflected his whole personality. A wide-nostrilled nose, heavy-lipped mouth and square jaw gave him the look of a determined and confident man.

"How long will you be staying, Jenna?" Greg asked her, as they ate their *gallo pinto*.

"My visa gives me two months, but I hope to be back in London within two weeks. Then, of course, if David, that's the producer, does decide to document your story, I may return with the film crew. Though I doubt that. He'll probably have another project for me on the other side of the world."

The peppers were hot, and Jenna quickly extinguished the burning in her throat with a glass of water.

"I should have warned you, *gallo pinto* takes some time to get used to."

"You should have." She nodded her agreement. "You're right though, it's absolutely delicious."

As their conversation continued and Jenna discovered more about her companion, she realized how much his character differed from the person she thought she would be meeting. Greg Oates was neither in his mid-forties nor an extremely boring intellectual.

Over their meal, which for her was breakfast, lunch and dinner, she questioned him in an effort to build up a background for her research.

"My favourite creature?" Greg pondered on his answer, taking a sip of orange juice before replying. "I guess it would have to be the leatherback turtle. It's an endangered species, and a fascinating one to study. I feel a very close second to that would be the quetzal bird. It is, to my mind and in the opinion of many people, the most beautiful bird in the world. Its home is in the jungles of Monte Verde, which is one of the places I intend to take you to, so, hopefully, you'll get a chance to see the quetzal yourself."

Jenna jotted his answers down in shorthand in her notebook.

"No — there's nothing else I would rather be doing. Natural history is my whole life. I love studying nature. My earliest memories are watching the fish in our garden pond. Though, as a boy, I did hanker to be a racing driver — an urge I've not really got out of my system." Greg laughed, a twinkle coming into his eyes.

"No, I'm the first in my family to become a professor. I'm even the first to have gone to university. My father was a factory manager and my mother a dressmaker. They were quite surprised when I took the career path I did. My father rather hoped I'd become a carpenter."

"No," was Greg's single-word answer to her "are you married?" But, like the rest of her questions, after a few seconds he enlarged on his reply.

"I've never met the right woman, though I guess that is most probably my fault; I allow myself very little social time. There was someone I was very fond of. We went to university together. Shortly after I moved to Costa Rica she met someone else. It was a good thing and I'm very happy for her, she married Jim, a sales rep. They live in Milton Keynes and have a very successful marriage. I'm sure it's much better for her than living out here, in the middle of nowhere, with me."

I'd question that, Jenna said quietly to herself, unsure as to what she meant.

Once their meal was finished they returned to the car-park and Greg's dilapidated estate car. The engine clattered and rattled like that of an old tractor before firing into life, then Greg drove back out on to the main road.

Dusk was slowly falling, bringing with it a cooler evening air, which lowered the temperature dramatically. As they entered the Puntarenas province, the dark night had arrived and the National Park Manuel Antonio's delights were hidden in blackness, as was the city of Quepos, a small urban sprawl which it took them only minutes to pass through.

The time passed quickly as Greg talked of his work with an enthusiasm that had Jenna deeply interested in what he said. He knew his subject well and made it come alive when he spoke of it, making Jenna eager to see the sea-diving pelicans, leatherback turtles and all the other wonderful creatures Greg had talked of.

2

THE bright headlights of the car picked out the small chalet-type bungalow in their beams. The building lay at the end of a long and potholed driveway along which the car was steadily making its way. Jenna was thrown from side to side in her seat every time the car hit a hole. She was glad she had adopted her usual habit of securing her seat-belt; it saved her from an injury.

"I'm sorry about the ride," Greg apologized as he tried to steer around the ruts and hollows in the road. "I keep meaning to fill in these holes."

He brought the car to a halt outside the little white-painted building, switching off the engine but leaving the headlights on, their strong beams lighting the way for Greg to enter the darkened building.

"Wait in the car while I go and turn the generator on so we have some light," Greg told her. "I don't want you falling over something in the dark. Unfortunately, mains electricity hasn't reached out here yet."

Within minutes, lights flickered on in each of the house's two front-facing shuttered windows. Greg came to the door, casting a huge shadow on the ground in front of him as he opened it wide to beckon her in.

Reaching in the back of the car for her suitcase, Jenna flicked the switch of the car's headlight's off. She stepped over the threshold of the cottage straight into the living-room, which was very untidy in the way of a bachelor pad. Greg cleared a space on the sofa to enable her to sit.

"Please excuse the mess, I'm nothing of a homebody. Maria, my housekeeper, normally keeps me in check, but she's away at the moment, visiting her daughter."

Jenna sat. It was very cosy. Though

thousands of miles away from his native land, Greg had furnished the room in the manner of an English country cottage. A comfy suite, wicker baskets and tables, with even a Welsh dresser to make the place feel like a home. It didn't differ too greatly from her own city apartment, which she had similarly consciously resolved to make as comfortable to live in as possible.

"You'll be staying in Maria's room. She'll be away for some time. Her first grandchild is due any day. She's thrilled to bits about it."

Jenna sat back and relaxed. It was the first time she had stopped travelling in many hours. She checked her wristwatch. It read six a.m., the time back home in London. She had yet to adjust her watch to the local time, which was six hours before Greenwich Mean Time — midnight.

"Would you mind if I retired for the night?" she asked him.

"I seem to be constantly apologizing for my manners," Greg gave a little laugh. "Please, feel at home here. It was a long drive into San José and back, so I think I'll turn in, too. Let me show you to your room."

Picking Jenna's suitcase up from the floor where she had put it, Greg carried it to her room, with Jenna following. They went from the sitting-room through a very poorly equipped, almost bare kitchen. There was no washing machine, dishwasher, microwave or even a proper cooker, but just a small camping stove. The next room was the housekeeper's room.

"Sorry it's so small," Greg said as he squeezed into the room between a single wardrobe and bed, with hardly enough room to turn around.

"Don't worry. I'm sure I'll be very comfortable in here."

The room was a luxury to Jenna. On several of her foreign assignments she had had to sleep sometimes in a tent, or airport lounge, and even, during a trip to Greece, in the back of an empty cattle truck. Though uncomfortable at the time, she consoled herself afterwards with the knowledge that without her little sacrifices she would not have been accepting, on behalf of the producer, the award for best documentary film at last year's film festival, for the documentary that resulted from her Greece trip.

"Tomorrow I'll start showing you around properly," he said, as he wished her a good-night before leaving the room.

Tiredness overwhelmed Jenna. Sitting down, she found she hardly had the strength to move, and fell back on to the bed in a deep peaceful sleep.

* * *

Jenna was hot. She couldn't stand it. Twisting and turning, there was no escape, it was as if she was trapped in a sauna; the air got thinner, her breathing more difficult. She gasped for air.

Waking quickly, Jenna opened her

eyes. Still fully dressed, she had slept soundly. The clock beside the bed read nine a.m.; she had overslept. The small room was starved of fresh air. In the wall above the bed was a window, which Jenna reached up to open wide, before taking deep gulps of the fresh, but clammy air.

Kneeling on the bed, she looked out of the window. Now, in bright daylight, she could clearly see the scenery that surrounded Greg's bungalow, which was situated on a small hill, a feature that she hadn't noticed in the darkness of last night. Below her window a path circled the house then wound its way down, bordered by ferns, dark green bushes and trees, over a rocky slope, to a beautiful white sandy beach, which was clear and clean, the deep blue Pacific Ocean lapping at its edge.

The view out onto the ocean was truly a beautiful sight, as Jenna shaded the bright morning sun from her eyes. The serene and picturesque view was so different to the one she saw each morning waking up in her Thames riverside apartment in London.

Not far out from the shore lay a solitary island — a tropical paradise. Just the sort of place Robinson Crusoe made his home, thought Jenna. From her vantage-point she could pick out the many and varied colours of its plant life.

* * *

Finding she was alone in the house, Jenna breakfasted. Greg had thoughtfully left cereals out for her, obviously thinking she wouldn't be prepared to eat *gallo pinto* for her first meal of the day.

Having changed into a short-sleeved blouse and skirt more fitting for the climate, she made her way down the path to the beach, from where she could hear the sounds of movement.

Once on the beach, Jenna slipped off her shoes, the fine sand warm and soft beneath her feet. Following the curve of the small bay, Jenna found Greg working on the hull of an upturned rowing boat.

"I hope I didn't wake you." Greg paused with a hammer on high, before bringing it down on a nail. Stripped to the waist, wearing brightly patterned surfing shorts, Greg looked up at her from his kneeling position by the craft.

"I wish you had. You must think me a terrible lazybody, sleeping so late."

"Nothing of the sort. I thought you were a very tired traveller." He focused his attention on the boat.

"You're a sailor, too, are you?" Jenna noticed the care he put into his work. Perhaps this was how he relaxed.

"Only out of necessity." He grimaced. "I'm afraid in my teens I got seasick on the Isle of Wight ferry. I keep the boat in good condition to get over to the island."

Jenna looked over to where he was pointing at the tropical island she had seen from her bedroom window.

"What makes it necessary for you to

go to the island?" she asked, aware of his displeasure about making the trip across water.

"It's where the largest colony of leatherback turtles lay their eggs," he explained, adding with a smile, "which you will discover tonight."

Gripping the edges of the boat, and lifting with his legs, he turned the vessel the right way up. As it landed sand flew up everywhere.

"Tonight?" she questioned, her hands brushing sand from her hair. "Why wait until then? Why can't we go now?"

"Because the turtles won't be there. They don't come up on to the beach until after dark."

Jenna felt silly at being so ignorant of the turtle's habit, although she couldn't be expected to be *au fait* with all the subjects of potential documentaries.

"That will be an important point to tell the producer," she spoke her thoughts. "The extra lighting needed to enable the camera crew to film at night will add to the cost of making the documentary."

Jenna sat on the largest of a cluster of rocks watching as Greg continued working.

"She sprang a leak on my last trip," Greg explained. "I'm giving her a long overdue waterproofing. We don't want to have to swim for home tonight."

"Which is just as well," Jenna laughed, confessing. "My swimming ability is not much above a doggy paddle."

"Don't worry, the *Marie-Anne* won't let you down."

Marie-Anne, I wonder if that's the name of his long lost love? Jenna thought. Maybe he named the boat after her.

Greg broke her train of thought. "I named the boat after my mother. I know it's silly, but every time I sail her, I feel closer to home."

"I don't think it's silly," Jenna answered him. She thought it showed him to be a sensitive man. Then, recognizing his sensitivity, she thought it necessary to explain her reasons for asking him personal questions yesterday. "I hope you don't think I was being nosey, yesterday. I was just getting background for my research."

Greg smiled understandingly at her.

"It's now my turn to ask questions," he said with a cheeky grin. "I have to get my own back, and I *am* being nosey," he added with a laugh.

As he spoke Greg continued working, opening a tin of what looked like paint, but was a liquid waterproofing, and brushed it thickly on to the boat.

"Fire away, then," Jenna challenged him in a friendly manner, "though I must warn you I think I'm a better interviewer than interviewee."

"OK. Are you married?"

"No."

"Then are you engaged?"

"Not now, but I was many years ago."

"I'm sorry it didn't work out." Obviously other people's happiness was important to him. "Is there any chance of you getting back together?"

"No." Jenna shook her head. "He moved away, we lost touch with each other. We weren't really suited for each other, which wasn't surprising. I was seven and he was nine years old."

Greg threw his head back and laughed, pointing at her with the brush. "You had me fooled there."

"Seriously, I'm not engaged. There is very little chance for me to form a relationship in my work. I never know from one week to the next where I'll be. Last year I was only home for five months, and that wasn't in one go. It's not a firm basis for a relationship."

"And if you weren't a researcher, what would you be?"

"I have no idea," Jenna admitted, "it's all I've ever wanted to be."

"Señor Oates!"

From above them, near Greg's bungalow, a male voice called out. It sounded to Jenna to be that of an old man.

"Down on the beach, Alberto," Greg

shouted back, as a man in his mid-seventies hobbled down the path toward them. A Costa Rican, the man was wiry and light of foot, but slowed by age.

"This is Alberto, my gardener, handyman and general helper. Without him I would be unable to get by. He has been my mentor since I took my first step on this soil."

"Alberto, *permitame que le presente a* Señorita Jenna Fervair."

"*Saludos*, Señorita Fervair."

"*Saludos*, Señor."

Once Greg had introduced them Alberto and Jenna exchanged greetings. Then in a rush of Spanish too quick for Jenna's unaccustomed ear, Alberto spoke to Greg.

Greg turned to her. "I'm afraid the plans I had for today have to be changed, I have to go into Tamarindo. There's a donkey about to go into labour. Unfortunately the family are too poor to be able to afford a veterinary surgeon, and as I'm the nearest thing I've partly volunteered and partly been conscripted to help out."

"Señor Oates." There was an urgency in the way Alberto spoke; despite their language barrier Jenna could sense Alberto was troubled.

"The donkey belongs to Alberto's son, and is a vital part of their livelihood. The birth is going to be a difficult one as the youngster is in the breech position." Greg picked up his tee-shirt and pulled it on over his head. "I could do with an extra pair of hands."

Greg had asked for her help, but not in a direct way, giving her the opportunity to refuse without feeling obliged.

"OK, then I'm your volunteer."

"Super." Greg patted her on the back, and in leaps and bounds they ran behind Alberto, back up the path.

A small pick-up truck was parked at the top of the cliff. It was in no better mechanical condition than Greg's estate car, and as Alberto slowly drove the truck away he proved himself to be a very poor driver. Within seconds he had stalled the engine.

Jenna and Greg sat on the bed of the truck, their legs resting against the dropped tailgate. As they travelled along the rutted tracks that passed for roads, Jenna was able to gaze in wonder at the scenery she had missed in the darkness of the previous night, finding it both beautiful and bewildering, seeing plants she had only previously seen in photographs.

"Costa Rica grows two main crops," Greg told her as they bounced up and down in the truck. "Up on the mountains the *Ticos* grow coffee beans, while on the lower land there's banana plantations."

A sudden cloudburst and torrential downpour had Greg scurry to a box just behind the truck's cab, from which he took a large plastic sheet. Coming back to sit beside Jenna, he held it over their heads, sheltering them from the rain.

"This is the biggest drawback of

living in paradise," Greg looked up at the now clearing skies. "Rarely a day passes without a rain shower."

Tamarindo bore little relation to any English village Jenna knew. It was closer to the sea than Greg's bungalow, and rows of fishermen's huts lined the shore. It was so picturesque that for a brief moment Jenna envied the peaceful life of its inhabitants. But she knew that she would soon become bored living in this remote village, being used to the metropolis and her busy way of life.

Tamarindo was lovely, Jenna decided, but as a holiday retreat, not a home. Alberto drove the pick-up through the village, where everyone seemed to know him and turned to wave as he drove past. It was a very friendly place.

"We're nearly there," Greg reassured her when he saw the discomfort she was experiencing. Riding in the back of a pick-up truck wasn't the most pleasurable way to travel.

As Greg finished speaking, Alberto stopped the truck outside a small cabin.

An air of poverty covered the area. Though it was neat and well kept by its inhabitants, they were obviously poor farmers.

Greg jumped from the rear of the truck before helping Jenna to the ground.

"Señor Oates, I so pleased you come."

A young Costa Rican man ran out of the cabin, grabbing Greg by the arm. Jenna took him to be Alberto's son. He had the appearance of his father. There was no time for formal introductions, as at a running pace the young man led Greg to the rear of the cabin, Jenna and Alberto following behind.

In a small stable, the floor covered with straw, lay a donkey, bellowing as the group arrived. Even to Jenna's untrained eye she could see the animal was close to giving birth, and in distress.

"There, there," Greg knelt beside the donkey, tenderly stroking and comforting it. In fast and confident Spanish Greg gave Alberto junior brief instructions, which he followed, by going out of the stable to return with water and rags.

For the next four hours, Greg struggled and worked hard in a desperate attempt to ease the donkey's discomfort. Jenna found she was not needed: the three men were fully able to cope without her. A hot sun shone down on the stable, bringing the temperature inside to an unbearable peak. Jenna stepped outside, cooling down in the shade of a tree. A weak bellowing, which grew louder and stronger, had her hurry back inside. On unsteady legs a small donkey tottered beside its mother.

"You are clever man, Señor Oates," Alberto praised Greg, an obvious relief coming across his face. "You save my son's animals."

"I forever thank you." Alberto junior's English was even more halting than his father's.

Greg sat, leaning against the wall of the stable; the delivery had been difficult, tiring him greatly.

"Does this sort of thing happen often?" Jenna asked, once the fussing around him by the Costa Ricans had eased down, and all attention was focused on the new arrival.

"Maybe once every few months, I guess. This is probably about my eighth birth. I've dealt with most minor ailments." He added, with a laugh, "Donkeys are becoming something of a speciality with me."

"So there's a possibility you could be called on while the film crew was here?" As always Jenna was looking for opportunities to improve on the documentary's story.

"There's always that chance." Greg got to his feet. "The villagers have a little way of their own of thanking me for delivering their young animals."

"Which is?" Jenna was intrigued.

"They name them after me." He answered. "There's a number of donkeys and goats trotting around called Greg.

"Though it won't be the case today," Greg continued, "the new arrival is a girl."

As they stepped outside, Greg stretched and yawned.

"You must be very tired," Jenna sympathized with him.

"I am."

"I'll understand if you want to call off tonight's plans to go over to the island."

"No," Greg shook his head. "We'll make the trip. I don't need any excuse to go over, I'd spend all my time there if I could."

"Señor Oates, I thank you again."

Alberto came out of the stable behind them, still expressing the family's gratitude.

In a response which Jenna had come to accept as part of Greg's nature, he brushed aside the older man's thanks. "I'm just glad I could be of help."

"We have chosen a name," Alberto told him. "We call her Jenna." He turned to Jenna, smiling. "For you, Señorita."

"I am very flattered." Jenna's response seemed to be what Alberto expected, and he left them, parting with a cheery wave.

"You've had a great honour bestowed on you," Greg ribbed her, "having a donkey named after you."

* * *

At night the beach was dark and mysterious, rock clusters lurked in the shadows like huge, prehistoric creatures. The beam from Greg's torch swept across the ground, lighting their way.

"Where's the motor?" Jenna asked, as she helped him pull the boat down the sand to the water's edge.

"There's no motor," Greg explained, hauling the boat into the water. "The sound of the engine would frighten the turtles away. We have to be very quiet. Manpower is what propels the boat across to the island."

"And womanpower," Jenna giggled. "I insist on helping."

"Fine by me," Greg told her, adding with a laugh, "I prefer to be a passenger, anyway."

"Equal power," Jenna joined in his fun. "I'm not doing all the hard work myself."

Greg threw his sports bag into the boat.

"Jump in now, Jenna."

Jenna scrambled over the side of the boat, before Greg pushed it into the sea; once the craft was afloat, pulling himself in. Taking an oar in each hand, he began to row toward the island. The sea was as calm as a park boating lake and the boat glided across it seemingly without effort. The warm sea lapped the fingers of the hand Jenna trailed over the side of the boat. Taking less than ten minutes from leaving the mainland, they landed on the beach of the island. With Greg, she jumped out of the boat, helping him to pull it up on to the sand.

Greg took his sports bag out of the boat, removing two torches, handing one to Jenna.

"Keep close to me, and don't switch the torch on until I tell you. The turtles aren't too far away, and we don't want to frighten them off."

Jenna stayed near to Greg as they left the beach to enter the thick, hot jungle that edged the sand. In the trees above, monkeys chattered, birds sang and creatures called to each other in the night. A full moon shone down, lighting their pathway.

Vines hung, slapping Jenna with their wetness. She brushed them out of her way, but the vegetation was so dense that soon the task overtook her and she gave up her fight.

"This place is really creepy," she made a half-hearted complaint to Greg.

Greg turned, raising a finger to his lips. "Hush, we're nearly there," he whispered.

They came out into an opening with a beach ahead of them. They had crossed the narrow island.

In the gentle waves of the ocean ahead, Jenna could see several large dark unidentifiable objects.

Silently, Greg lay flat on the sand, reaching into his sports bag to take out two pairs of binoculars.

"Jenna," he whispered, then pointed to the ground, indicating she lie beside him.

On the dark, hot, uncomfortable island, Jenna lay down as if it were the south of France and she were on holiday and sunbathing.

"Here," he handed her the binoculars, "keep them trained on the water's edge."

Her elbows in the sand, propped up on her arms like a bird-watcher, she looked through the glasses into the sea.

Slowly, the previously indistinct objects emerged from the ocean, crawling up the beach, and Jenna could now clearly see they were the leatherback turtles Greg had described to her. She gasped at their size, hundreds of times larger than a pet tortoise, being at least six feet long, almost the dimensions of a small car.

Jenna counted a dozen turtles. Further down the beach there were more. She found herself holding her breath in awe at the wonderful sight she was witnessing. Jenna's fingers tightened around her torch. Greg put his hand over hers, shaking his head.

Now, only a few feet in front of them the turtle nearest to them began to dig with its rear flippers, until a small hole soon appeared. Once the turtle had dug to the depth necessary, it backed to lay its eggs one by one into the waiting nest.

"OK," Greg nodded, switching on his torch, the beam focusing on the turtle as she laid her final clutch of eggs. "We can't disturb them now."

Jenna turned on her own flashlight, at the same time moving up from her prone position on to her knees. The sand, made wet by the earlier shower of rain, stuck to her clothes, making it fortunate that she was wearing chain-store off-the-peg blouse and slacks. The sticky grit would have ruined a one-off designer outfit.

"I don't know if it will be possible for a film crew to transport all their equipment through there," Jenna nodded back towards the jungle. "Is there any other way round?"

Greg thought for a while before answering. "Not while the turtles are nesting. But they could land this side of the island earlier in the day, without the turtles even knowing they are here."

"I think that's the best idea," agreed Jenna. "I will have to tell David that."

The beam of Jenna's torch concentrated itself on the now departing turtle.

"We'd better start getting back," Greg said, after they had spent an hour watching all the turtles leave the beach and return to the ocean. "We have an early start tomorrow."

"We do?" Jenna questioned him, as

they stood, preparing to make their way back to the beach.

"I thought you would like to visit the Volcan Irazu."

"Where?" Jenna laughed, she still wasn't conversant with Spanish names.

"It's Costa Rica's volcano."

"Volcano!" she gasped. "Surely that's a place to stay away from?"

"You've very little cause for worry," he assured her. "It hasn't erupted since 1978."

Jenna stifled a giggle, she wasn't sure whether he was joking or not with his reassurance.

The journey back through the jungle was neither as long or as laborious as the trip going the other way had been. No longer was there a need to be silent, and where previously the breaking of a trodden-on twig would have alarmed the nesting turtles, Jenna was able to walk with freedom.

"Let me row back to the mainland," Jenna asked him. "I did promise to do my equal share."

"All right," Greg reluctantly agreed, adding the rider, "but you must let me navigate; go wrong out in the ocean and you could go hundreds of miles off route."

Once on the beach, when they had pushed the boat into the water, Jenna jumped in and settled herself with an oar in each hand. She had never rowed before, but she thought it couldn't be too difficult. Circling the oars above the water, Jenna waited for Greg to get into the boat before she dropped the ends of the oars into the sea. Moving her hands in a circular motion, she began to propel the boat.

Greg didn't seem too perturbed by her first attempt at seacraft, and settled back to make sure they were heading in the right direction.

"Are you navigating by the stars?" Jenna asked him, impressed by what she thought were his astronomical skills.

"I'm not," he confessed. "I left a light on in the house. I can just see it from here."

Jenna was getting into her stride, rowing the boat steadily so that she wouldn't tire herself out.

"You're going a little off course," Greg told her, "you want to bring the boat to port."

Port? A slight panic ran through Jenna. Not only did she have no idea which was port, she didn't know how to bring the boat to it. Greg obviously thought she was experienced on the water.

"To port, Jenna," he repeated, possibly thinking she hadn't heard him the first time he had spoken.

"Which way is port?" She whispered the question in a hesitant manner, half not wanting him to hear, yet knowing that he must.

"The left, you want to bring the boat to left." He made his instruction clear.

"And how do I do that?"

"Don't you know?" Greg asked in disbelief.

Jenna shook her head, then realized

he couldn't see her in the semi-dark. "No."

"This isn't the ideal time for a boating lesson," Greg half-heartedly complained, "but you may just as well learn, though I must admit I never saw you as a novice. You started off very competently."

Jenna lifted both oars out of the water, as Greg started to give her instructions.

"Now put just the oar in your right hand in the water and row."

Jenna found she was unbalanced just rowing with one hand: as she concentrated the boat started to turn but sharply, not gradually, and in an attempt to straighten it out Jenna dropped the other oar into the water.

"No," Greg shouted, not in alarm but startling Jenna. She released her grip on the oar in her left hand and it fell into the ocean. Within a split second, Jenna brought the right oar over the side and into the boat and dived for the left oar, her fingers just missing it by inches. She got to her feet to stretch out further for the oar, but she wasn't accustomed to the rolling of the boat on water and hadn't yet got her sea legs. As she reached out for the oar she lost her balance. The boat began to move beneath her.

It was the coldness of the ocean that was her first shock. Then swiftly the realization of her situation hit her. She was drowning, taking gulps of the salty water as she desperately kicked out with her legs and tried to paddle with her arms, but panic made her movements uncoordinated.

"Greg." Her voice was weak, she called for him, in the darkness she couldn't see the boat.

"Jenna! Jenna! Jenna!" She could hear him shouting for her.

She went under completely, but a combination of strength and the determination to survive had her come back to the surface, the air welcome on her face.

The beam of the torch, like some

giant spotlight, swept across the ocean. The boat was far away, the current having dragged her some distance.

Slowly Greg scanned the ocean, then the light hit her, a blinding white beam picking her out.

"Hang on. I'm coming," Greg shouted. Then Jenna heard a splash as he dived into the sea from the boat.

Jenna went under again, coming back up quickly, splashing out with her hands to hit Greg's shoulder as he came swimming towards her. She grabbed for him, her fingers tight on his clothing as she went under again, dragging him with her.

"Let go," Greg told her. Her panic would drown them both.

As she released her grip he turned her on to her back, cupping one hand under her chin and, in a life-saving manner, pulled her back toward the boat.

Jenna grabbed the side of the rowing boat as Greg heaved her up into it. Coughing and spluttering and breathing heavily, Jenna lay gasping on the floor of the boat.

An oar landed beside her, with Greg following it into the boat. He turned her on to her side, pressing the middle of her back. Jenna found herself expelling bitter sea water.

"You took in about half the Pacific Ocean," Greg tried to lighten the situation with humour. "How do you feel?"

"Terrible." Jenna groaned; she had never felt worse. She was nauseous, her eyes stinging, her mouth dry, and she was soaked to the skin.

3

"I'M sorry," Jenna made her rather weak apology when they got back to the mainland.

Greg upturned the boat on the beach, sea water drained out. The bottom of it had been awash.

"Don't worry. It was an accident." Greg was more than understanding, which was very good of him Jenna thought, considering that the whole incident was entirely her fault. "There's no damage done."

"Just maybe a little to my pride," Jenna confessed humbly. The wet clothes clung to her and she longed to change out of them. At least, she chuckled to herself, the horrible gritty sand had been washed out of them.

Greg led the way back up to the house. With every step she took Jenna's clothes squelched and they weighed heavy on her. Still shaking a little from her shock, Jenna was pleased to get to the bungalow and into a warm bath.

"Feeling better?" Greg asked as Jenna came into the sitting-room in a bathrobe. She had washed the sticky sea water from her silky hair, leaving her feeling refreshed.

"Much better," Jenna thanked him as she took the seat he indicated at a dining-table. "And how about you, how are you? You know now you're something of a hero to me, having saved my life."

"I'm just pleased I was there, anyone would do exactly as I did," he answered modestly. He too, had changed from his wet clothes, and had prepared supper for them.

"From the age of eight to eighteen my New Year's resolution was always — this year I'm going to learn to swim — but I'm afraid I never succeeded," Jenna told him, laughing at her own shortcomings. "I have the skill to type sixty words a minute, yet not the ability to save myself from drowning."

"It's never too late to learn," Greg told her as he placed a full plate on the table in front of her. "I'm not much of a cook I'm afraid. Maria looks after that sort of thing."

"It looks absolutely delicious," Jenna surveyed her meal. "Fish is one of my favourite foods, and I love white bass."

"I caught them earlier today," Greg said, as he began to eat. "I've no freezer, and in this heat things don't stay fresh for long."

"You have a very basic lifestyle," Jenna commented, but not critically.

"I don't need anything that I don't already have," Greg answered. "I've no television. I wouldn't have the time to watch it. There's no radio, telephone or anything that I would consider a luxury. I don't need them."

"Don't you ever get bored?"

"Bored!" Greg exclaimed with fake alarm. "Never. Though I must say that having you here has been enjoyable for me, spending time with someone from my own country has been a change."

"You get homesick, then?" Jenna picked him up on what he said.

"You are twisting my words," he smiled. "I didn't mean I get homesick, though I'd be a liar to say I didn't. On a Saturday afternoon while I'm knee-deep in mud, or struggling through a wet jungle, sometimes I wish I was home, walking down to the ground with a group of friends to watch City play, or maybe just enjoying a pint in the local. But that's the price I pay to be able to do the work I love; most people aren't that lucky."

"No, they're not," Jenna agreed with him, realizing for the first time how their lives were on a parallel. She had sacrificed a lot for her own lifestyle, but not for one moment had she regretted it. "You must get away from your work at sometime, so how do you relax?"

"Spare time is very difficult to find,

but when I do, I go surfing. There's a great surfers' beach a couple of hundred miles down the coast, but I haven't been for ages." Greg began his meal. "As I said, leisure time is sparse."

They ate their meal in silence. The fish was the best Jenna had tasted in a long time. She had last eaten such a delicious meal at a tiny family-run restaurant in a Cornwall fishing port at the beginning of last year, when she had visited an old schoolfriend who now lived with her husband in Truro.

Their dinner finished, Greg cleared the table, refusing her offer of help to wash up.

"You go to bed. I'm used to this heat, but it is tiring to someone new. You need your rest more than I do, and you need your strength for tomorrow."

Wishing him good-night Jenna retired. Once in bed she thought over the day's events, a cold fear running through her as she recalled her moments of panic as she fought in vain to save herself from drowning. Had it not been for the swift action of Greg Oates, she should surely now be in a watery grave, a thought that filled her with terror.

From the next room she could hear the clinking of crockery as Greg put away the dinner things. Jenna was then hit with an emotion alien to her, a self-sufficient person: a feeling of security that Greg was nearby, close to her and there to protect her. Jenna tried to expel these thoughts from her mind, but they stayed with her as she fell into a deep sleep.

* * *

"Bananas for breakfast?" Jenna giggled. She unpeeled the fruit's skin as she sat in the passenger's seat of Greg's car as he was driving to Volcan Irazu. "What's wrong with your much loved *gallo pinto*?"

"You've never tried to eat *gallo*

pinto in a moving car," Greg, good-humouredly replied, as, briefly, he took both hands from the wheel to remove a banana skin. Fortunately they were the only vehicle on the deserted road. "There's nothing wrong with these. I picked them fresh this morning. They are full of the nutrients and vitamins you'll need over the next few days."

"I will." Jenna's agreement was treated as a question by Greg.

"Yes, after we've visited the summit of *Volcán Irazu*, I thought you might care to backpack into the jungle of Monte Verde. The best way to get to know that area is to camp overnight, then you really feel part of the jungle. I don't intend to go far into the jungle, maybe three or four miles, but in the terrible heat it'll feel more like thirty or forty."

Greg concentrated on his driving as they approached the city of San José, through which they had to pass on their way to the volcano. "Whatever discomfort you feel because of the humidity of the place I guarantee you'll think it's worth it when you discover the beauty of the jungle."

"I should get my first sighting of the quetzal bird." Jenna knew, and was pleased, she could impress him with the fact that she had absorbed what he had told her earlier.

"I can see why you are employed as a researcher," Greg made his compliment sound as if it was merely a comment. "You have a retentive memory and good observation."

"I think I have more of a love of my job, than anything else," Jenna tried not to sound egotistical. "Everything else falls into place when you enjoy your work."

Greg sped through the city with the same style of driving as he had displayed when collecting Jenna from the airport, this time sticking to narrow back roads; there was no need to go through the centre of the city so they by-passed it.

Even though it was only five a.m., the

best and only comfortable time to drive according to Greg, San José was alive and busy. Like East End costermongers setting their market stalls up early the *Ticos*, the Costa Ricans' own term for themselves, were preparing for a day's busy trading. Both men and animals drew their heavy barrows through the streets. The shouts and laughter of San José residents filled the air with merriment, their happiness spreading to Jenna, who, despite her early rising, was wide awake and full of vigour.

Greg knew the streets of San José just as Jenna could find her way around London's West End, taking short cuts through lanes, roads and alleyways that were only just wide enough to take a car.

Out of the city the mountain-like volcano stood in front of them. A road wound its way up one side, and from Jenna's viewpoint it disappeared at several points into dense areas of forest.

Greg pointed the car in the direction

of the volcano's summit, pushing the accelerator pedal to the floor. The car, coughing out exhaust fumes, made its way up the side of the mountain. A drizzle began to fall on the windscreen, gradually increasing to a heavy rain, and Greg switched on the windscreen wipers of the car, which fought to clear the glass against difficult opposition.

Rain carried mud from the coffee plantations down on to the road, on several occasions causing the car tyres to lose their grip, and beneath them the wheels spun, fighting to find firm ground under their tread.

Greg held the steering-wheel tightly as it threatened to break away from his hands. Following the rain came a thick fog, which had Greg switch on the car's lights, their yellow beams hunting through the heavy mist. The weather had changed from a beautifully clear morning to conditions akin to those on a Scottish moor in mid-winter. The only thing that remained consistent was the now stifling heat.

"I wouldn't have thought you would suffer from fog in paradise," Jenna laughed, as she spoke to Greg over the roar of the slogging engine's rattles and groans.

"This isn't fog," he answered, "but low cloud. For most of the year the summit isn't visible from the ground."

As they spoke, an old Chevy truck came hurtling around a sharp bend towards them, at considerable speed. Greg only had seconds to take evasive action to avoid a collision.

"Road hog!" Jenna made a weak protest. Turning to Greg, "Did you get his number?"

"I had the opportunity to get the whole truck," Greg joked. "But no. I didn't. Why?"

"We should report him for dangerous driving," Jenna answered. "He could have his licence taken away."

"He wouldn't even have a driving licence," Greg told her, as he reversed the car out of the low bank he had driven into. "The guy behind the wheel was no more than ten years old."

"Ten!" Jenna exclaimed. "He wouldn't be able to reach the brake pedal."

"Which is probably why he was driving so out-of-control." Greg found the whole situation to be humorous. "The entire lifestyle in Costa Rica is totally different to that in Britain. Here the family is normally the only workforce on huge banana or coffee plantations. It's very difficult for the farmers to survive financially, so they have to take all measures they can to save money."

Feeling humble, Jenna didn't say anything more on the subject. She concentrated on the scenery as they came out of the cloud into a dry and clear day. The distance between the sharp turns became shorter and shorter, and the bends more acute.

Jenna looked at her watch. It was half an hour since they had begun to climb the volcano and they were still a long way from the summit.

They drove through the centres of

small, mainly agricultural villages and through farms, pausing occasionally to let animals cross the road in front of them.

"We're about a mile from the summit, now," Greg told her as they drove into another spate of thick cloud, which caused the windscreen wipers to work hard again.

As suddenly as it came, the mist disappeared, leaving the car to take its last bend before Greg brought it to a halt. Ahead of them were the three giant craters of the *Volcán Irazu*.

"Wow!" Jenna gasped, slipping the seat-belt off to get out of the car, while Greg switched off the engine to produce a relieving silence.

"Despite all my travels I have never once seen a volcano," Jenna confessed as tentatively she made her way toward the craters, her earlier keenness having been superseded by a feeling of caution.

"It gives you a sense of being on top of the world up here," Grey remarked as he joined her in a steady stroll to the craters.

"The last time it erupted was '78?" Jenna wanted confirmed what he had told her before.

"Yes." Greg nodded.

Jenna gingerly approached the crater closest to her, looking over the precipice and down to where, over 2,000 feet beneath her, gurgling spitting fire of red-hot rocks and lava roared away. Jenna could feel her face growing pale as she surveyed this awesome wonder from which came a heat that had her in a near-faint. She drew back from the crater. The heat it generated had caused a strong thirst in Jenna, her mouth and throat were bone-dry.

"You should never travel far on a hot day without carrying spare water," Greg told her, as they walked back to the car. He opened the tailgate of the vehicle, taking the lid off a cool box, to remove two plastic bottles of water, closing the lid on at least two dozen bottles still left untouched.

The water was cool and refreshing to Jenna, and after they had drunk, Greg took the empty bottle from her, putting it into a box in the rear of the car.

"These can be used again," Greg tapped the bottles. "I'm a strong believer in recycling. I know plastic isn't the best of materials, but glass doesn't travel well."

"You're involved in the green revolution, are you?" Jenna asked as they got back into the car. They quickly wound the windows down, as the inside of the car was baking-hot.

"I've always been something of a conservationist." Greg started the car. Performing a three-point turn he headed the car back in the direction they had come. "I hate having to throw away anything that pollutes the world. I loathe it every time I have to drive this. But getting anywhere in Costa Rica is near-impossible without personal transport."

They drove back down the side of the mountain, the incline so severe that

Greg had to continually hold the car back on its brakes, as well as keeping it in a low gear.

It had been a long journey to make, to spend only ten minutes at the craters when they had arrived. Yet the outing had been worth the discomfort of the extreme heat, just to experience the wonder of the volcano.

Jenna began to cool as they drove, a humid but welcome breeze coming into the car.

"I guess it would be worth my while having air-conditioning installed in the car," Greg told Jenna as they wound their way down the volcano. "But I doubt I normally use the car more than twice in a fortnight. I rarely travel far. So, economically, it doesn't seem a wise idea."

Jenna agreed with his logic, while privately thinking that the installation of an air-conditioner would probably double the value of the car in one bound. She imagined the 'rust bucket' wasn't worth even £100. It was a miracle to Jenna how the car kept running, for there seemed to be a danger of breakdown at every revolution the engine made.

"My car has air-conditioning." As soon as she had spoken Jenna wished she could retract it. She feared it sounded like she was boasting, so she quickly added, "Though it came as standard." A statement which made her original sound worse.

It now seemed as if her car was a top-of-the-range expensive model, which, in fact, it was. Jenna was in high-paying employment and apart from her apartment and luxury BMW motorcar, she had few valuable material possessions. Jenna could fully enjoy neither her car nor her flat, as she spent so little time at home in London and rarely used the car in the capital city itself. During the rush hour the journey from her Chelsea apartment to her Covent Garden office, a distance of under two miles, could, if she drove, take her at least an hour.

Using public transport, either over or underground, she could normally complete the journey in a third of the time.

"I doubt you have much use for air-conditioning in the normally wet British weather," Greg laughed. "Though I imagine it's handy for trips abroad."

"Yes." Jenna didn't contribute to the conversation any further. She could have told him of her last holiday, when she and a couple of friends from the company had driven across the continent to Italy. But Jenna was aware that even her most innocent of remarks could appear to be bragging.

To Jenna, Greg's opinion of her was extremely important. She didn't want to present an image of a self-important, wealthy and even slightly egotistical career girl. Normally, Jenna wasn't concerned what people thought of her. She preferred to be liked, which made an assignment much easier, but her primary thoughts were for the project in hand to be successful, with making friends a bonus. This assignment was different. The story was, as usual, her first concern, as Jenna was always dedicatedly loyal to A.Z.T. Associates — they had made a substantial investment in her for this project and she remained one hundred per cent loyal to them. But, in almost a schoolgirlish manner, she desperately wanted Greg to like her. Greg respected her both professionally and personally, he had on several occasions displayed his admiration for the work she did and her skilful handling of the delicate subjects she sometimes became involved with. It was possible to respect someone and not like them, though she was sure Greg didn't hate her, for such a thought would be complete nonsense. There was a scale she applied to all her relationships, from one to ten, with one being merely an acquaintance. It was closer to the other end of the scale that she would like to place Professor Greg Oates.

"You've gone quiet." A look of

concern spread across his face as he turned to speak to her, his mirrored sunglasses reflecting her image, the shades he wore for comfort, not as she had suspected on first meeting Greg, as a symbolic expression of forced style. "OK, are you? Heat not wearing you down?"

"No. I think I am close to getting used to it." Jenna smiled. "Though when I leave here I hope my next assignment isn't in Alaska, that would really muddle my body temperature, going from boiling to freezing."

"It's coming up to midday, so we should really be getting out of this hot car and into somewhere cooler."

"Then it's not true what Noel Coward said about mad dogs and Englishmen?" Jenna laughed.

"I can't speak for all the others," Greg drove the car off the hard road on to a dirt track. "But certainly this Englishman likes to get out of the midday sun."

As soon as the car stopped Jenna

alighted, relieved to be out of the oven-like conditions. She found a shady spot under a nearby tree, sitting with her back resting against its trunk. Even wearing the minimum of clothes, shorts and a short-sleeved blouse, Jenna felt over-dressed. The tree offered only a little shade and that couldn't be described as cool, only slightly less hot than the direct sunlight.

"Have you ever thought of getting a convertible?" Jenna asked him, considering that a soft-top car would be much more comfortable for travel in this extreme heat.

"I nearly did have a convertible," Greg joked. "Coming out of San José a few months back a truck driver almost took the roof off. He'd misjudged a manoeuvre, and was making an awful job of correcting it when I came along. The old car might not be much to look at, but its brakes could stop a charging elephant, fortunately for me, and I was able to avoid an accident. Seriously though, a convertible would be impractical because it rains here every day, so I'd be constantly lowering and raising the hood."

Removing his hat to use as a fan, Greg sat beside her, leaning back against the tree.

"We're not that far from Monte Verde." He closed his eyes, resting after a long drive in an uncomfortable climate. "It should only take us a couple of hours to get there. Maybe we'll go half a mile into the jungle and pitch camp for the night. We should be settled by midnight."

"I didn't see you pack a tent this morning." This was Jenna's roundabout way of asking if he had forgotten it. Just before dawn she had, under his guidance and instruction, packed a haversack for herself, including a single set of cutlery, a sleeping bag and a few other essentials. Taking as little as possible was the main rule to stick to. In an area where one pound could feel like ten, packing an extra bar of soap could make a great deal of difference.

"We don't need a tent," Greg told her, without once opening his eyes. "The jungle of Monte Verde is really too hot for a sleeping bag. But I like a few of my comforts, and don't relish sleeping without any sort of bedding."

The place where Greg had chosen to stop was peaceful, despite being only a few metres from a main road, which was used only occasionally, and then by an oxcart or other animal-propelled vehicle. It was so quiet that Jenna found she was falling asleep, and felt unable to resist the sensation as she grew more and more tired.

"Hey. Sleeping Beauty. Wake up! We have got to be going."

The voice aroused Jenna from her sound sleep. She slowly regained consciousness, stretching her arms above her head, at the same time yawning heartily. Greg had been calling her. Eyes open, Jenna saw him standing by the car. She looked at her watch: it was nearly two. She had been asleep for over an hour.

Sleeping Beauty, he had called her. Was she taking his words too literally, or had this merely been a touch of humour? Or was there a deeper meaning behind them? Jenna didn't know.

"I didn't know I was so tired." Jenna got into the car beside Greg. The interior of the vehicle had cooled drastically now that the peak of the day had passed.

"In this heat it creeps up on you." Greg understood how she felt.

"I hope I've not delayed the trip to Monte Verde." Jenna realized her falling asleep may have affected his plans.

"Don't worry. I wasn't intending to be there at a fixed time, anyway."

Greg started the car, pulling out on to the road and toward Monte Verde.

4

DUST flew up everywhere as the car bounced along a rough track. It was as if they were at the centre of a storm, but then the dust died away as they came on to a hard road, and the wheels ran smoothly along the flat surface.

Already they had driven ten miles off the main road to Tamarindo, continually travelling eastward, with the edge of the jungle of Monte Verde now only two miles from them.

"We'll leave the car near to the hotel. Just for security. Like everywhere else in the world, one can never be too cautious," Greg explained his plans to her, "and then set off. We won't get too far before the daylight fades, but late evening is one of the best times to walk."

Since leaving the main road they

had not met a single vehicle and it wasn't until they pulled up outside the boarding-house that they saw other people. Jenna unloaded their haversacks from the rear of the car, while Greg went in search of permission to park it.

Greg's haversack was at least twice the weight of her own, as he had insisted on carrying all their cooking utensils and food, refusing to share the load with her, in a gentlemanly fashion. Though they would only be camping out for one night, they needed to take with them a lot of fluid, for it would be disastrous not to have enough water with them.

"Everything sorted out?" Jenna asked Greg on his return.

"Sure. No problems."

Greg lifted up Jenna's haversack so she could put it on, pushing her hands through the straps as if she was putting on a coat. It needed a little adjustment to fit comfortably. Though she was aware of the backpack, it wasn't a great weight.

Greg pulled on his own haversack and, thumbs tucked under the shoulder straps to spread the weight, led Jenna off towards the heart of the jungle.

"Let me know if you get tired," Greg told her. "You have to take things easy, and not go beyond your normal level of endurance."

"I will," Jenna assured him. She was sensible enough to know not to overdo anything.

The hardwood trees that towered high above them, their long branches almost touching as they reached out to cast huge shadows down on to the ground, became denser as they went from the sparse edge of the jungle deeper into it. Like on the turtles' island, thick vines hung down, slapping their moistness against Jenna's face and body. In the wet and hot atmosphere, the ground beneath their feet was soft mud, on which Jenna slipped and slid with each step and caught hold of the vines, using them to steady her.

"Is it like this all over?" Jenna found

walking difficult, as at times the mud was ankle-deep, swallowing her shoes.

"No. Only in places."

The 'places' seemed to extend for long distances, there rarely being any hard ground. Jenna was beginning to feel tired; walking was becoming a strain; she needed a rest, just a few minutes, then she would be refreshed enough to continue.

"Can we take five?" she asked Greg, who was marching on in front of her, seemingly oblivious to the difficulties. It was as if he was on a hiking trip in the New Forest. There wasn't a bead of perspiration on his forehead.

"Of course." Greg slipped off his haversack, placing it against a tree, where he suggested she sit.

"Phew! It's quite a struggle!" Jenna's legs went weak, only able to carry her the few feet to sit down. "How far have we come? A mile, a mile and a half?"

"See that tree up ahead?" Greg pointed into the distance. "The large one standing alone."

"Only just." The tree was so far away that it was only just distinguishable. "Why?"

When we reach that, we'll have come a quarter of a mile."

"Only a quarter of a mile?" Jenna could hardly believe it. Her legs felt like they had carried her miles and miles. "And we've not got anywhere near that yet."

"We go left at that tree and on for another quarter of a mile to a clearing. There we will set up camp for the night."

Jenna was amused by Greg's terms. At home she would give directions such as 'turn left by the chemist then right at the traffic lights', whereas Greg's landmarks were trees and clearings; he had obviously adapted well to his surroundings.

"Getting your strength back?" Greg asked Jenna. He was eager to get going again, but didn't want to hurry her before she was ready.

"Give me a minute longer and I'll be bouncing around like a three-year-old," Jenna joked, rubbing her legs furiously to re-start her circulation.

"Look! Look!" Greg shouted like an over-excited child. He was pointing to the treetops. "Look!"

"What is it?" Jenna wondered what he had seen, was it a UFO? He was insistent that she see what he was watching.

"It's a quetzal bird."

"Is that all?" Jenna sat down again, having leapt to her feet when he had first shouted. "I thought you had seen a flying saucer."

"I'm sorry," Greg calmed, apologizing. "It's just I'm a little eccentric where the quetzal is concerned, and was eager for you to see him. He's flown away now."

"I understand." Jenna's remark made him feel better. His cheeks had reddened with embarrassment when thinking he had made a fool of himself. "Why did we have to come out into this place to see the bird? Isn't there a private collector in the city?"

"There are private collectors, but no one has a quetzal bird." Greg sat down beside her on his backpack. "They don't survive in captivity."

"How tragic." Jenna was saddened by this thought. "Why not?"

"I don't know," Greg admitted. "But the *Ticos* believe they die of a broken heart. To the Central American people the bird is a symbol of freedom."

"I didn't know the bird was the centre of such attention."

"Oh yes, it's regarded quite highly. In fact, both the ancient Aztecs and Maya worshipped it as the Quetzalcoatal, which means the feathered serpent."

"You know your subject well." Jenna was impressed by his knowledge.

"I'm sorry — I've bored you." Greg was very apologetic. "I must learn that not everyone shares my obsessions."

"No, please, don't stop. I am interested, and even keener to actually see a quetzal." Jenna was hoping to have the opportunity to spot the bird soon, its history made it fascinating. "Tell me, what does it looks like? I don't want to miss one by not recognizing it."

"You won't do that," Greg smiled. "You can hardly not notice one of these beauties."

"What size is it? Bigger than a sparrow? Smaller than a parrot?"

"It's four feet long," Greg began.

"Four feet!" Jenna exclaimed. "What is it? A giant among birds?"

"No. Well," Greg smiled," maybe I should explain. The quetzal is four feet long if you include its three foot tail plumes."

Jenna laughed. "I thought I'd be looking for something the size of a small aircraft. I've been puzzling how a bird with a body weight equalling that size could perch in a tree."

"The quetzal is a beauty and very graceful. In fact, it's poetry." Greg looked skywards again in the hope that he could spot once more the bird he had just seen. "Are you rested?"

Jenna nodded, she was ready to begin walking again. During her respite she had prepared herself mentally for the journey that lay ahead. Being psychologically fit for the walk was as essential as strong physical ability.

Greg stood, holding out his hand for Jenna to take, helping her on to her feet, then reached down to pick up his haversack, swinging it up on to his back, as if it were as light as a feather.

"We haven't got that much further to go," Greg told her as they began to walk. "Would it be easier for you if I carried your backpack?"

"No." Jenna was insistent. "I mean, no thank you. You've already enough to carry. I don't want to burden you with more."

They continued walking, with the tree that marked a quarter of a mile getting gradually closer. Jenna was becoming accustomed to the effort needed in the difficult circumstances.

Using all her strength to pull her feet up out of the mud to take the next step, she was fortunate in having strong legs. She owned a mountain bicycle, and, when the opportunity arose, would take to the country hills on it. The exercise had strengthened her legs and improved her stamina. Jenna planned, later in the year, to take a cycling and camping holiday in Wales, confident in the knowledge that the Welsh mountains would be like a pleasant Sunday outing in comparison to backpacking in the jungle of Monte Verde.

"Oh, no." Jenna sighed. Her shoe had become stuck in the mud, and lifting her leg up had left her foot bare. On one leg, stork-like, she tried to keep her balance as she nearly toppled over.

"Here, let me do that," Greg came back to Jenna, seeing the predicament she was in. He knelt down beside her, his bare knees sinking into wet mud. "We can't have you taking a mud bath."

With a sharp tug, he pulled the shoe from the mud, holding it out for her to slip her foot into.

"Try that for size, Cinders." He held the shoe tight, then secured the laces so that it wouldn't come off again in the mud.

"It fits," Jenna laughed, continuing his joke. "Now, Prince Charming — you'll have to marry me."

Greg returned her smile. Was there an extra twinkle in his eyes? Or had she imagined it?

"Don't move, Jenna." Greg whispered an urgent warning.

Jenna stood rigid, not daring to breathe. The hairs on the back of her neck prickled. What was it? Was danger near? Keeping her head still she moved her eyes from left to right, up and down. She could see nothing out of the ordinary. The past few seconds seemed like minutes. There was a tickle on her nose, could she afford to move and scratch it? Jenna didn't take the risk. She remained motionless.

"What is it?" she asked in a hushed voice.

"There's a quetzal bird, just above you, on the right."

Moving slowly, as not to panic the bird into flight, Jenna turned to look. There, perched on a branch, hidden when she had looked previously, was the most beautiful bird she had ever seen.

"Greg, it's wonderful." Jenna was in awe of the creature. Its chest feathers were metallic green in colour, beneath which its abdomen was a vivid crimson. The bird's plumage resembled a rainbow. Jenna had no doubts, this was certainly the most beautiful bird in the world. It was like a giant parrot whose colours were brighter and more vivid than any other she had ever seen.

Greg placed a hand on her shoulder, looking past her at the quetzal bird.

"You know now I wasn't exaggerating in my description." He kept his voice low.

The quetzal was either unaware of or undisturbed by their presence and continued preening himself.

"It is absolutely lovely. I can see why it was worshipped." Jenna smiled as a thought came to her.

"What is it?" Greg wondered what was amusing her.

"I was thinking of the difficulties involved in filming in this jungle," Jenna answered. "It's so hot and muggy. It will take some arranging."

"So the documentary is more than a possibility?" Greg tried to cajole her into saying more than she had already.

"I told you before, Professor, it's not my decision." Jenna considered that the use of his title would bring their conversation back on to a solely professional level, temporarily suspending their relationship from any friendliness.

"I'm sorry. It's just that I'm eager to get the wildlife of Costa Rica to a wider audience." Greg was very apologetic. "It was wrong of me to harass you."

The quetzal flew away, making it unnecessary for Greg to make the difficult decision to move on, enamoured as he was by the bird.

"Don't think that I am angry." Jenna thought she had better explain herself. She wanted to explain clearly her position to him, not wanting a rift to come into their, up to now, easy and relaxed relationship.

"It was the first time since we met that you have called me Professor," Greg smiled. "I feel chastised. Like a schoolboy who's done wrong."

"Shall we go on?" Jenna was eager to move, both to call a halt to their conversation and to cool. Standing still made her feel even hotter.

"Of course."

It was another half-hour before they reached the clearing Greg had spoken of: a small round piece of hard ground, no more than seven feet across, set in the middle of an oasis of soft mud. It was like a castle surrounded by a protective moat. Dusk had fallen in the last few minutes, and it was in semi-darkness that Jenna slipped off her backpack, before seconds later removing her shoes. Mud was caked on them. Drying hard, it cracked, falling away as Jenna slapped the trainers against the ground.

Jenna was pleased to see Greg removing tin cans of food from his haversack. She had developed an appetite during their trek and was keen to satisfy her hunger. Most of their meal would need heating, for which purpose Greg had brought with him a small primus stove. Setting the stove up in a safe place, clear of any vegetation that could accidentally catch alight, he began to cook their meal.

"Can I help?" Jenna offered her assistance, which Greg politely refused.

"There's not a lot to do, fortunately."

The aroma of the cooking food had Jenna's hunger pangs increase.

"I'm no chef," Greg admitted, jokingly adding, "though I doubt the best cook in the world could do a lot with bangers and beans."

Jenna ate heartily, consciously slowing her eating. So hungry was she that without thinking she would have hurried instead of savouring her food and not fully enjoyed it.

"I think we should settle down for the night as soon as we've finished," Greg suggested. "I know it's still early, but we need all the sleep we can get. Tomorrow will be much harder, as there's a lot more I want you to see, and that will be further into the jungle. And it's unlikely in this heat you'll get that much sleep, so just resting quietly will go some way to redressing that."

Taking Greg's advice, Jenna got her sleeping bag from her backpack, snuggling down into it on the leeward side of a tree. She felt even hotter than earlier, but as the hours passed the extreme heat cooled to a pleasant warmth, leaving her comfortable enough to ease into sleep.

"Sorry. Did I wake you?" Greg

walked past Jenna, his movement disturbing her.

"No. I wasn't asleep." Jenna had awoken earlier, keeping her eyelids closed in the hope that she would fall back into unconsciousness. "What time is it?"

"Just before five."

Jenna hadn't realized the night had passed and morning arrived. Slowly she opened each eye, the bright early sun flickering through the branches of the tall trees dazzling her. She had slept without interruption for at least six hours, a feat that she would have considered impossible in the difficult conditions of the jungle.

"You are up and about early," Jenna remarked as she rubbed the sleep from her eyes, yawning and stretching, welcoming the new, fresh day.

"I'm surprised he didn't wake you."

"Who? What wake me?" Jenna's mind was clearing of sleepy thoughts and coming to life.

"This little chap." Greg came back

to her side, a small feathery body cupped in his hands.

Jenna sat up in her sleeping bag to take a closer look at the bird Greg was holding. It was obviously a youngster, its feathers still a fluffy down. The tiny bird was squawking in a voice alien to it, a shout that would have been more suited to a bird twice its size.

With a single finger, Jenna stroked the bird's head. She felt a sticky substance on her skin; it was blood. She drew her finger away quickly, fearing she had hurt it.

"What happened to him?"

"A predator got to him. Brave little guy put up quite a fight. His attacker got tired and left him for dead. Luckily I found him."

"You can save him?"

"I'll do my best. And with a bit of help from nature he should be OK."

Greg took the chick over to where his backpack lay, removing a small medical kit. Jenna was impressed by his gentleness with the small creature as he tenderly cared for and soothed it. The squawking died down to be replaced with a quieter chirp as Greg treated the injured bird.

Jenna scrambled from her sleeping bag. She had slept fully dressed both because of decency and because the thin and light clothing made little difference to her body heat. There was no opportunity to cool down by undressing.

She knelt down beside the cross-legged Greg. "Is there anything I can do?"

"You could hold him while I inject some antibiotics." Greg held the trembling little bird out for her to take.

The chick wriggled in her hands, but she held him tightly. To release him back into the wild now would be sending him to his death. He soon became exhausted, his tiny heart beating fast. Jenna could feel every thump through her fingers.

Greg took a syringe from the first-aid kit, filling it with a liquid from a small vial.

"Keep him still," Greg warned. "I don't want to accidentally inject you. You'll be flying around the treetops."

Jenna smiled at Greg, amused by his joke.

"Don't worry." She spoke to the bird. "The nice man is going to make you better."

"There. That should do the trick." Greg emptied the syringe.

Already the bird seemed stronger. It began to peck at Jenna's fingers with its sharp beak.

"Do I let him go now?" She wondered if the bird was fit enough to fly away.

"No. Keep hold of him. He'd only get a few feet before collapsing." Greg put away his medical kit. "My guess is he was plucked from a nest. We need to find that nest and return him to it."

Making sure the bird wouldn't get

free, Jenna handed it back to Greg's caring hands. Greg got to his feet, looking up at the treetops.

"I found him over there." Greg nodded into a dense part of the jungle. "I doubt the nest is far away. Predators don't usually take their victim far."

"Nature can be so incredibly cruel," Jenna commented, thinking of the small, defenceless bird, which so narrowly had escaped being a bigger creature's breakfast.

"I'm afraid that's the way of things," Greg replied thoughtfully. "This chap's predator will become the victim of something else and so on."

"The law of the jungle," Jenna remarked, without realizing the pun she had made.

"I'm afraid so." Greg stroked the bird's head. "Let's get you home."

"How are you going to get him back up to his nest?" Jenna wondered; the nests she could see were at least sixty feet up in the trees.

"I'll climb," Greg stated, slightly

surprised that she should be puzzled.

"Isn't that dangerous?" Jenna looked up again, the trees were extremely high and appeared to be treacherous; the slippery vines would hamper instead of aiding an ascent.

"No." Greg tried to sound confident, though Jenna could tell there was a slight apprehension behind his outward assurance.

"Can I help?" Jenna was eager to be of some assistance. She didn't want to stand by while he possibly risked life and limb. "Could I maybe guide you from the ground?"

"The best thing you can do is stay here and not venture outside of this hard ground area." Greg told her. He was insistent that she do as he said, as he left her. For a time he was within her sight, but as he went further the vegetation became thicker and Greg was no longer visible to Jenna.

She stood waiting for his return. There was nothing else for her to do. Jungle noises carried on around her, the chattering of monkeys, squawking of birds and the cries of other animals, the sound of the wildlife an eerie music that was serenading her.

There wouldn't be any harm in making a brief exploration of the area around the camp site, Jenna thought. In the dusk of last night she had no idea of the features around their chosen sleeping place for the night. Greg had told her to stay put, but she could see no problems in taking a look around, she wouldn't go far and would be back before he returned, leaving him none the wiser.

Jenna put on her trainers, tying them tightly with a double knot. She wasn't going to lose them in the sticky mud today.

A few feet away from the hard ground the soil beneath her feet began to soften, at first to a tacky mud, then degenerating to a barely solid ooze. As though an increased gravity was pulling on her legs, Jenna sank into the mud, which soon extended above her knees. It felt like quicksand. Jenna stayed calm, aware that to panic would only serve to increase the danger of moistness glistening in the early morning sun. Jenna quickly weighed up the opportunities she had of freeing herself. There were few. She could struggle, try to extract her legs, which could possibly cause her to sink deeper. Should she fail, then Greg wouldn't be gone too long. She could wait for him to return and rescue her. In one single action she would destroy the respect he had for her and prove that she was unreliable. He had told her not to move, and she had ignored his warning. Alternatively there were the vines. If she could just stretch far enough to grab them, Jenna knew she could pull herself out of trouble. She would only have to reach out a few inches, it wasn't that far. Jenna was sure she could grab the vines at her first attempt.

She tried to steady herself, which was difficult because she was standing in a substance as slippery as ice. She relaxed her arms, fear making her muscles tense. She needed to be lithe like a cat. Jenna stretched out, extending her arms above her head, with the vines almost within her grasp. She was almost there. Her fingertips made contact. Just an inch more and she would catch hold of them. There, she had done it. As if she was climbing a rope Jenna pulled herself up, her shoulders and upper arms hurting as, slowly, her legs were released. Hand over hand, Jenna drew herself up the vine, her grip tightening as its wetness threatened to make her slip.

She kicked out, her legs were finally free. But she still wasn't safe. Now she was hanging from the vines while beneath her remained the treacherous mud. All she had to do was to swing on the vine; the momentum would carry her over the hard ground. Judging her timing carefully, she could drop down to land safely. In theory it seemed simple, in practice Jenna found it difficult. The strength was rapidly fading from her arms. She couldn't hold on for much longer.

From her feet upwards, Jenna began to swing, her whole body swung, but with no rhythm. Her feet went forward while her knees went back. Jenna remained stationary. Now her hands were slowly slipping down the vines. She desperately fought to find the will to cling on, but it was close to impossible. Refusing to give up and fall back down into the mud as her grip went, she used every effort to throw herself clear of the mud.

Jenna leapt, but her jump was too short — she landed in the soft mud. Scrambling fiercely, she tried to get out of the swamp, almost succeeding, but, at the last moment she staggered sideways. Instinctively Jenna threw out her arms in an attempt to regain her balance, failing which she would use her hands to break her fall. Jenna landed on her side in the mud, rolling over as she hit it like a parachutist trying to save herself from injury. The world began to spin, Jenna couldn't stop it, faster and faster it spun. Unable to stop herself rolling, Jenna covered her head with her arms, shielding her face from the prickles and thorns that threatened to scratch her skin as she fell through them. Finally Jenna came to a halt, her body hurting all over. Jenna lay still, taking stock of her situation and trying to discover where exactly she was. Knowing that when she fell from the vines she had slipped into the mud and had apparently toppled over a precipice, Jenna looked up from where she had landed in soft undergrowth. Shading her eyes from the brilliant red ball of fire that so early in the morning was bringing a tremendous heat to the jungle, Jenna estimated she had fallen twenty feet. She recognized that she was fortunate that her tumble had been in a soft area where, apart from a few scratches, she had no injuries.

Lying partially on her left side, partly on her back, Jenna realized she had to climb back up the almost vertical face that confronted her, to get back to the camp site. She raised herself to a sitting position before managing to stand. The ground underneath her feet was solid mud, shaded from the sun by the precipice above it, and held her weight firmly.

She chastised herself for venturing away from their camp. Not for the first time was she angry with her own actions. Now Jenna was wishing she had stayed put stuck in the mud, and had not foolishly tried to free herself, a manoeuvre which had led to the situation she now found herself in.

Was there another way up? Jenna wondered. For the first time she looked over the tall bushes that she had landed in, hoping that she was positioned somewhere near an easier ascent. What Jenna saw shocked her. She hadn't, as she had previously thought, landed on the jungle's floor, but had, and the realization had her sway in a semi-faint, fallen on to a narrow ledge of a sheer cliff. Beneath her was the familiar slimy muddy ground; between it and her was a drop of at least seventy feet. Had she fallen to the right by just a matter of inches, that was where she would now be.

The climb back up to the top hadn't appeared easy before, but now, with the realization of what lay beneath her, and knowledge that a single slip would cause her to fall, the climb looked impossible. A tear came to Jenna's eye; why had she been so foolish? Had she waited for Greg to return, they would probably now be eating their breakfast, or all ready to leave for the day's trek. Where was Greg now? Was he still trying to find the nest and return the bird to the security of its home? Or had he returned and found she was missing?

Not one for self-pity, Jenna wiped the tears from her eyes. It was she who had fallen, and it was she who would have to find a way out of her predicament. It dawned on Jenna that she was headstrong, her character was one of ‘shoot first — ask questions later’ — she would act before thinking, and on several occasions it had caused her problems. She had once assured her producer that she could find a certain piece of film footage concerning Indian elephants that he required urgently for a documentary, without planning where she could secure the film and had failed miserably. Such was her eagerness for success as a researcher. She had, after some time passed, put this incident down to her youth and inexperience, but now realized it was a flaw in her character that she needed to correct. Luckily, a colleague had known where she could obtain the film she needed, saving her face and, more probably, employment.

Jenna was about to make the same mistake again, deciding to climb back up without considering either the pros or cons of such an action. It was the chilling discovery of the huge drop that lay beneath her which brought Jenna to her senses. She would have to swallow her pride and call out to Greg for help. She knew that he quite rightly would probably be exceedingly angry.

The jungle was coming alive with noise as its inhabitants awoke. A host of sounds reached her ears. Twitters, warbles, squeals and whistles filled the air. Jenna had the real fear now that Greg would not hear her call for help, such was the din that she had to compete with. He should have returned to the camp site by now, discovering that she was not there. Greg would almost certainly be looking for her. Maybe she should stay put and wait for him to find her, though she had no idea how long it would take, or whether he would even consider looking for her where she was.

"Greg!" she shouted. All around her the jungle's inhabitants reacted to her call. Startled birds flew from their perching places. Small animals scampered away through bushes, and large creatures ran through the undergrowth.

Drawing air in through her lungs 'til they were at bursting point, she expelled it into a loud shout. "Greg!"

"Jenna. Where are you?"

Hearing Greg's voice immediately reassured Jenna. She was no longer facing her predicament alone.

"Greg! Over here!" she called in response to his shouted question.

"Where are you, Jenna?"

"Over here!" Jenna shouted again, trying as hard as she could to raise her voice.

"Where are you?"

Greg had become more distant. His voice quieter. He was going away from her in his search. Evidently he had not heard her cries for help.

"Jenna." She could barely hear him, which fuelled her fear that he wouldn't find her. How could he, if he was looking in the wrong place?

Jenna shouted again, and again until her voice became hoarse and all she could emit was a tiny croak.

5

NEARLY an hour had passed. Greg had still not found her, or had he come even remotely near to where she was. She could easily believe that he would never find her, such was the difficult terrain he was searching. Would he carry on until nightfall precluded all chance of discovering her? Would he go back to the boarding-house where they had left the car, at least half a day's trek, and ask for the help of other people in his search? All sorts of different thoughts and possibilities ran through Jenna's mind; some sensible, some irrational and others downright stupid. Had the strength of the sun's heat and lack of water addled her brain? Jenna considered that if she was rational enough to think of this possibility, then it wasn't so.

The situation had come to a point where now she considered that the only person who was going to rescue her was herself. She had not fully accepted this, but weighing up all other chances, including that of Greg finding her soon, she realized that it was truly the only option open to her.

At the front of her mind was the thought that, should she at any time slip during her treacherous climb, she could fall the seventy feet or so to certain serious physical injury, or even worse. Raising herself steadily again to her feet, Jenna, inching sideways with the concentration of a tightrope walker, moved along the five-feet length of the ledge. She could see no footholds, jutting rocks or strong roots that would support her climb. The sheer precipice was covered with vegetation, most of it slippery, thin strands of leaves and weak twisted branches. There wasn't even the opportunity to start her climb. Going back up seemed an impossibility. One other, less attractive option was open to her, however, and now there was no real alternative. Jenna couldn't go up, so she would have to go down.

Where would she be if her descent was successful? Jenna wondered. The only thing she knew for certain was that she would be in a different part of the jungle to Greg, and even further away from him. Whether she would be safe or not was another consideration. There would no longer be the risk of her falling, but what dangers would there be? Jenna wasn't capable of finding her way out of the jungle, one tree looked very much like another, and she could go round in circles without knowing. Or could go miles deeper into the jungle.

It was this thought that had Jenna decide to stay where she was. At least, by staying put she wouldn't hamper her own rescue. Her mouth was dry and her throat began to feel sore. A strong thirst was building in her. It was eight hours or more since she had last taken in water, and Jenna wasn't that ignorant of the jungle not to know that she needed liquid. She could not risk becoming dehydrated.

Moisture was all around her in the shape of the vegetation that grew everywhere. But was it safe to quench her thirst by chewing the leaves of these strange, and for all she knew, poisonous plants? Acutely aware of the warnings she had received as a child not to eat wild berries, she applied an adult's brain to the dilemma. Jenna would not be consuming the plant, merely taking the wetness from it. If they were poisonous she doubted that absorbing such a small quantity could seriously harm her.

She broke a leaf off a plant that grew close to her. Before putting it in her mouth she smelled the leaf first. There was a faint, distasteful aroma, but its chief smell was of wet vegetation, a cross between that of freshly cut grass and an early morning dampness.

It tasted tangy and bitter, and Jenna

removed the leaf from her mouth quickly as a hotness spread over her tongue. Jenna's attempt to quell her thirst had only served to increase it, making her more distressed than before.

"Jenna. Are you OK?"

The voice from above startled Jenna because she had grown accustomed to being alone and almost resigned to not being found.

"Greg." Jenna was able to speak his name despite the soreness of her throat. She looked up to return weakly his wave, as he looked over the edge of the plateau above her. She was delighted to see him. Her urgent desire was for a drink. "Water," she gasped.

Greg was, Jenna thought thankfully, like a good boy scout, always prepared. He had water with him, and with careful judgement slid its plastic bottle container down to her.

The water was cool and refreshing, and she emptied the bottle without once removing it from her lips. Her thirst had only been physically uncomfortable and she was in no danger of any permanent harm.

"What happened? Are you hurt?" Greg's initial words expressed concern. Outwardly he showed no annoyance at her.

"I slipped and fell." Jenna kept her explanation short. She would tell him the full story later. "I'm fine."

"Don't worry. I'll get you off there." Greg's reassurance wiped away all her fears. She could rely totally on him. Inwardly she was amused as he, before hurrying away, added an unnecessary, "Stay where you are."

Greg wasn't gone long, returning within minutes, a length of thin cord wrapped round his arm and shoulder. He tied the rope around the trunk of a large tree, securing it before tossing the remainder down towards Jenna.

"You always carry this with you, do you?" Jenna called, her voice regaining its strength. She was amazed that he had the rope so readily to hand.

"It's light and easy to carry — you never know when you need it," Greg answered as he leant over the precipice, wriggling the rope to free it from bushes that it had caught upon.

Jenna wasn't sure of Greg's plan of action; did he expect her to climb up the rope? She doubted that she would be able to, especially when considering the huge drop that lay beneath her — Jenna had difficulty keeping her mind off the possibility of falling. Greg soon answered her unasked question.

"Keep to one side. I don't want to bump into you as I come down."

He was coming to her rescue. This was a relief to Jenna.

Gripping the rope, Greg swung his legs out over the edge. With the method and skill of an abseiler he was shortly beside her.

"You were lucky to land on this ledge." Greg spoke quietly without over-dramatizing her good fortune. He stamped his foot on the ground. "It's a good solid one, too. Most of these types of ledges crumble under any sort of weight."

Jenna found that her body was trembling through fear. It was only now as her ordeal was coming to an end that she realized how serious a danger she had been in.

"Surely you're not cold?" Standing beside her Greg could feel Jenna shaking, and was puzzled as to why it was.

"No, of course not," Jenna replied, not wanting to admit how nervous she was. Greg was self-confident and had shown a degree of bravery in, without a thought for himself, climbing down to her.

"How are we going to get back up?" Jenna didn't want to appear to be sceptical, but how they were together going to make the ascent worried her. "I'm sorry, Greg, but I can't climb the rope."

"It's easy," Greg tried to convince her, "just hand over hand. But don't worry, you don't have to climb. I doubt you'd have the strength at the moment."

"Then how . . . ?" Jenna didn't have the chance to finish her sentence.

"Piggy-back." Greg preempted her question. He smiled broadly as if it were all a game.

Jenna was just able to stop herself bursting into a nervous laughter. His suggestion seemed so comical. But she could see it was really the only logical solution to the problem.

"The last time I did this was at a schoolfriend's birthday party at least fifteen years ago," Jenna giggled, as she, Sinbad-like, climbed on to Greg's back. Joining her hands at the front of his neck, she clung to him, feeling more than a little self-conscious.

Greg's strength surprised Jenna. He didn't seem to be under any extra strain as he began to climb, hand over hand, a vice-like grip on the rope. At no time did Jenna fear he would slip. His movements were positive. She had complete confidence in him and his abilities. Jenna knew now that it would have been impossible for her to make the ascent alone, especially without the aid of a rope.

Through the thin material of Greg's shirt Jenna could feel the movement of his muscles in what seemed like an effortless climb. She was tempted to look back now that she was near safety. It was as if she was mocking the drop that had failed to claim her when Jenna turned her head, eyes flittering across the scene below. A cold shiver of fear ran through her and she clung even tighter to Greg, causing him to call out in complaint.

"Hey, steady on. You're strangling me."

Jenna apologized, releasing her grip slightly, but she still securely held on to him.

They were near the top, with the last point proving to be the most difficult of the ascent. The passing from the rope over the jutted piece at the top proved to be near-impossible. Greg dug his feet hard into the mud, using them in his bid to carry them over the last obstacle.

Up safely, Greg found a small section of hard ground to come to rest on. Only now did he show any sign of tiredness by panting a little which, considering the physical effort he had just used, was only a small indication of his weariness.

"You can get down now," he told her gently, aware that she was still clinging to him as if her life depended on it.

In truth, Jenna didn't want to let go. The fear she had experienced would last her a lifetime, and for a few brief moments was feeling emotions normally alien to her self-reliant character. She wanted to be held.

"Sorry." Jenna released her grip on him, delighted to find hard ground beneath her feet once more.

"Is that sorry for wandering off from the camp site?" Jenna could detect a note in Greg's voice that hadn't been there before. It wasn't anger but disappointment, bitter disappointment in her.

"It's sorry for everything." Jenna tried to look him directly in the eyes, but her overriding feeling of guilt had her avert her gaze.

"I knew something like this could happen," Greg appeared to be blaming himself. "I should never have left you."

Giving regard to Greg's current state of mind, Jenna felt it best if he, for the time being at least, remained ignorant about her having become stuck in the mud.

"It's all my fault." Jenna was big enough to admit that she, and she alone had been in the wrong. "You told me not to move, and I ignored your warning. I fully expect you to lecture me."

"I'm not going to do that," a warm smile crept across Greg's face. "In your position I would have done exactly the same thing."

"I'll never do anything like it again,"

Jenna promised. "I have certainly learnt my lesson."

"Good." Greg reached out to take hold of Jenna's shoulders, his large hands very gently shaking her in a friendly manner. "You have caused me to miss my breakfast. So, how about a mid-morning snack?"

"I can think of nothing better," Jenna agreed. Her hunger had taken second place to thirst.

Their breakfast was made up of an identical meal to supper — bangers and beans. To Jenna it was a feast, with her appetite surprising her. They sat side by side to eat.

"Under the circumstances I don't think we should carry on, but go back," Greg told her after they had finished their meal.

"I've spoilt things, haven't I?" Jenna wanted a direct answer. She didn't want him to shilly-shally in his reply.

"What is there to spoil?" Greg had a question of his own. "All there is to see is jungle, and more jungle."

"But you had plans." Jenna would have felt easier in her mind had he been infuriated with her. She had learnt that Greg was too relaxed in his lifestyle to let anything bother him.

"Another time," Greg insisted. "We can come here another time."

Even though it was all her fault, Greg was doing his utmost to make Jenna feel better. There would never be another time, they both knew that, Jenna would soon be flying back to England. In a week's time she would probably be gone from Costa Rica.

"Once more I owe you thanks for saving my life." Jenna realized she had a great debt to Greg Oates. "I seem to have become accident-prone around you."

"I hope you're not blaming me," Greg laughed. "I'd hate to think that I'd brought you bad luck."

"I see you as something of a lucky charm. You came to my rescue both times."

"Let us hope there won't be a third,"

Greg wished. "Though they do say things happen in threes."

"I was never very superstitious," Jenna confessed. "Though if I was I would put down my recent incidents to walking under a lot of ladders."

"We'll take a steady walk back to the car," Greg suggested. "There's no need to tire you out further."

"Tire me out!" Jenna exclaimed with a laugh. "I was lying still doing nothing, it was you who wore yourself out trampling all over the jungle looking for me."

"I'm just pleased I found you." Without speaking one more word, Greg leant across and kissed her on the cheek, his lips warm and gentle, sending a tingle through her.

Puzzled, Jenna turned to him. She wasn't angry at the liberty he had taken, secretly she was both pleased and flattered.

"What was that for?"

"As I said, I'm pleased that I found you."

"Wouldn't words have sufficed?" She tried to draw him out and succeeded.

"Simply words couldn't have told you how I felt."

Standing, Greg prepared to leave, his change of mood so sudden and severe Jenna was beginning to doubt their brief kiss had actually happened and it wasn't a figment of her imagination. Knowing it had been real, she knew there was only one reason for Greg's present actions. He, like her, was sensing that far deeper feelings had begun to infiltrate their relationship. His mood swing meant he was trying to fight them, to struggle against a ruthless and strong enemy which could strike without warning — love.

* * *

Jenna bathed and changed into clean clothes. Arriving back in Tamarindo, Greg had dropped her off at his bungalow before heading into the village. That had been nearly four hours ago, and he had not yet returned home.

Alone, and with time to relax, Jenna searched Greg's many and vast bookshelves for light reading material. His store of books didn't include the latest in paperbacks, or even any fiction. Virtually all of his private library consisted of hardback reference editions, mostly concerned with flora and fauna, offering her encyclopedic facts but no light relief.

A particular collection caught Jenna's eyes. Three volumes lined up side by side, each sharing the same author — Professor Kim Oates. Obviously Greg had several strings to his bow, including literary ones. Each of the books featured Costa Rica in their titles.

Taking one of the books from the shelf, Jenna settled down on the sofa intending to read Greg's *The Wildlife of Costa Rica*, while awaiting his hopefully soon return. Though she would learn more about Greg's favourite subject through his written words nothing, for Jenna, could replace his actual presence.

During the time they were now apart, Jenna thought deeply about the emotions she was feeling toward Greg. She had a fondness for him which she was sure could, in time, develop into something much stronger. Greg was attractive and she was drawn to him. But Jenna was intelligent enough to know that true love wasn't something that could, as many believed, happen at first sight.

Love needed time to be cultivated and a relationship built upon it. Jenna knew she would, if she spent much more time with him, fall in love. It wasn't something that *would* arise however. She would soon be on her way back to England and then on to another assignment. Within a month, with all that Jenna would have to occupy her in her employment, Greg would be nothing more than a distant memory. Or so she thought. What she *felt* was something completely different.

From outside came the crunch of tyres upon gravel and the rattling sound of the engine of Greg's car. There was silence, then the car's door banged shut.

"I'm sorry I was so long." Greg came into the bungalow, apologizing profusely, his arms full of large paper bags that apparently contained food. He hurried into the kitchen, calling to her from there. "I had several errands to do. Then someone left a message for me, I had to telephone them back, that alone took me all of an hour."

Putting the book down, Jenna went to the kitchen door. Greg was unpacking groceries like a suburban husband.

"What's all this?" Jenna asked, picking several cans up, each containing delicacies, including tinned peaches. "I thought you lived simply, only caring for your basic needs. These foods are comparatively exotic."

"I thought a good meal would make a change," Greg parried her question with a huge smile. "After all I have a special guest."

"You do?" Jenna wondered if the person he had telephoned was coming to stay. "Who?"

"You, of course." He replied, moving her gently out of his way. "There's something I left in the car. I got it especially for you."

"You shouldn't . . . " Greg was gone before Jenna could finish her sentence, " . . . do anything special for me."

Greg was in a buoyant mood. It was Jenna's opinion that he, too, had realized the course their relationship was taking and unlike her, who, for purely professional reasons, wanted to steer their friendship away from romance, was going 'full steam' ahead.

Greg came back into the house, the smile across his mouth indicating that he was delighted with what he had to share with her.

"It's only on loan, for the time you are here," he gabbled the last few words as if he didn't want to say them. "I hope it brightens your days up."

Greg held out a radio to her. Ancient, only one step away from the old valve-type, its age was given away by its size, almost twice that of a modern transistor, and constructed out of bulky wood instead of plastic.

"That's very thoughtful of you." Jenna was pleased. She had been feeling like an outcast from society in not knowing what was happening in the world. Now, at least she could hear the daily news.

"I'll get back to preparing our meal."

Greg returned to the kitchen, while Jenna remained in the sitting-room, tuning the radio to the World Service, only to discover she had missed the news report.

"Can I help?" Jenna offered her assistance in the kitchen where Greg was busying himself.

"I think I've got it all under control," Greg answered. He waved a recipe book in the air. "I borrowed this as well. You go sit down and relax, you've had a tiring couple of days."

"If you're sure," she asked him. "I like to keep busy. I'm not one that likes to be waited on."

"You'll have to get used to that tomorrow."

"What is happening tomorrow?"

"I've been invited into San José to give a talk at the university. I hope you'll agree to come with me. It's short notice, I know."

"I'd be delighted to come. I'm most impressed by your lecturing at a university."

"It's not that impressive." Greg was humble. "I submitted a thesis for a project they were doing a year or so ago. They've asked me to come tomorrow to be questioned on a couple of points. I hope you won't be bored by it."

"I'm sure I won't be." Jenna was confident that she would enjoy the sojourn in San José and the opportunity to see Greg Oates in a different light.

"Don't worry. We won't be roughing it and camping out tomorrow night," Greg opened a bottle of wine. "We will be staying in a four-star hotel."

6

"I'M sorry. You do understand, don't you?" Greg Oates asked her as they stood outside the centrally-situated hotel. The modern, tall construction dominated all the smaller, ancient and in some cases, almost derelict buildings around. "Why don't you spend the afternoon sightseeing, or perhaps shopping? I expect you would have soon got bored coming along with me. I'll meet you back here in the lobby about seven, we can eat, then go on to a theatre."

Greg stepped out into the busy road to hail a cab, having left his elderly estate car parked in the lot behind the hotel. He didn't want to arrive in his own car at the university, where he would have to drive in circles in search of a spot to leave the vehicle.

"I'll book seats for a show," Jenna

suggested, "and make a reservation in the hotel's restaurant."

"Great idea," Greg called, as he got into a taxi, his mind so occupied with thoughts of his lecture that he had little consideration for anything else.

"Good luck." Jenna waved as the cab pulled out into the stream of traffic, soon being swallowed up in the heavy flow.

Jenna did understand. Presenting a talk at the university was a huge step in Greg's career, but wasn't really a subject that her documentary would feature, as it would focus on his work with the wildlife rather than solely his work. He needed to go alone, with nothing that would affect his concentration. And she, according to Greg, would take his mind from the job in hand.

Going back up to her hotel room, directly across the corridor from Greg's, Jenna recalled her pleasant surprise when she had, less than an hour ago, answered the knock of the door, to find

Greg, ready to leave for the university, smartly dressed in a man-about-town three-piece suit, a plain shirt and dark tie encapsulating the image of elegancy.

"I wouldn't have recognized you," Jenna had laughed, as they took the lift down to the coffee shop together.

A visit to the hotel's resident barber had reduced the length of Greg's dark locks, and he now sported a more conventional hairstyle. Previously his wavy hair, which added to his look of a beach bum, would have caused shocked heads to turn in the café where they took refreshment.

"My mother would be delighted if she could see me now," Greg joked. "I think she doesn't believe I actually own a suit."

Jenna felt proud to be sitting with Greg. He drew many admiring glances with his strong, athletic physique combined with handsome features. Standing over six feet tall, he stood out from all the other men in the coffee shop, and Jenna herself received many envious looks at being Greg's companion.

Later, when back in her room, Jenna looked through the local tourist guidebook's listing of theatres. Finding a show that she thought they would both enjoy, she made a call on the direct-dial telephone at her bedside to the box office, booking two seats for that evening's performance.

After making a reservation for two in the restaurant, Jenna left the hotel and went out into midday San José. Her last few days had been spent in semi-solitude, and the vast number of people jostling along the pavements of Costa Rica's capital came as a sharp contrast. Walking a hundred yards made her feel as if she was being carried along amid a huge crowd of football supporters on their way to the Cup Final.

Several times she ducked into shop doorways to take a break from the bustling multitude. Standing apart gave her the opportunity to study the people as individuals instead of *en masse*. San José's residents were exactly the same in nature as the populace of any other of the globe's capital cities. Each person was involved in their own world, women were shopping, alone or with friends, men went about their work, with cab, truck and delivery drivers each fighting for a space on the crowded roads. Children were on their way to or from school, or playing their normal street games down alleyways or anywhere there was room to draw a hopscotch pattern.

Keeping law and order in the thronging city were *caballeros* on horseback, their steeds placid and even relaxed in the midst of blaring horns, revving engines and the general hustle and bustle of city life. The Caribbean midday rush was twice as, if not more, hectic than the London rush hour, and it was with bated breath and a cautious step that Jenna ventured from the safety of a doorway into the hurly-burly, immediately regretting her decision as half-a-dozen street pedlars came her way. Her pale skin and unhurried air targeted her as a tourist. Offers of necklaces, bangles and even small furry creatures, which she failed to identify, came her way.

"You buy necklace, beautiful Senorita. You buy."

"Bangles, bangles, you want? You want buy?"

With a shake of her head, and confident walk, Jenna passed the pedlars by. She knew that to pause or speak to them would involve her in a series of haggling episodes, and she wouldn't be free of them until she made a purchase.

Jenna had several hours to pass until she met up with Greg, so, with a map of the city centre in her pocket, Jenna decided to explore San José. On her list of sights to see were Costa Rica's National Museum, National Theatre and National Art Museum. During her first drive through the city, Greg had pointed out these buildings to her, and now she intended to take a closer look.

* * *

Exhausted by her afternoon's tour of the city, Jenna arrived back at the hotel at six o'clock. The cab she had taken from the Art Museum had been held up for half an hour in a massive traffic jam. Two streets away from the hotel she had abandoned the car and walked the remaining distance.

Desirous of a shower, Jenna felt dirty from exhaust fumes, her hair felt heavy with smog, and her skin gritty; she longed to wash the grime away. The baths she had taken in Greg's home were far from satisfactory, so old and rickety was the bungalow's water system. It was impossible to obtain a constant stream of hot water. After running for less than a minute, it would first splutter then dribble to a halt, causing her either to bathe in tepid water or a very shallow bath.

Basking in the shower, Jenna felt clean again, the hot jets of water stinging her skin.

The telephone rang. Grabbing a towel, Jenna stepped from the shower.

"Your call has been put through to London," the hotel receptionist told her, referring to a call Jenna had placed immediately on getting back. After several clicks and ear-hurting crackles she was through.

"Hello, David. Jenna here."

"Jenna, how are you doing?"

The call had the effect Jenna wanted, it made her homesick. She was, she felt, likely to get too comfortable in Costa Rica and too attached to Greg if she didn't remind herself of the other world that existed for her.

"I thought I would phone with a progress report."

"Good, I'm glad you did. I've been wanting to reach you," David began, "as there's another project that needs your urgent attention. I couldn't think how to contact you, staying as you are in the back of beyond."

It annoyed Jenna that David criticized the country without even having visited it.

"There is civilization here," she tried to stop herself snapping at him. "There are houses, not just mud huts."

"I'm sorry." David was taken aback by her stand for a foreign country. He hadn't been expecting it.

Jenna realised she had overstepped the mark. David was merely making a friendly comment, and had not meant to offend. Indeed, the remark should not have caused her to take offence.

"Things are going well here," she told him.

"Great, you can soon leave then?" David paused, Jenna could hear the rustling of papers on the other end of the telephone line. "I've been in touch with a zoo in Canada, apparently they are trying to re-establish the captive animals in the wild. It looks so interesting I was reluctant to send anyone else, I thought it best to wait to hear from you. I'll fax you all the information and you can fly up from Costa Rica."

"Can't you send someone else?" Jenna could hardly believe it was she who had spoken. The words came straight from her heart, not her mind.

"Someone else?" Her producer blustered. "Sure, I can send Penny. But Jenna, I thought you would enjoy the project."

Jenna had to quickly think of an excuse as to why she was unable to fly to Canada. Jenna could hardly tell him the true reason, that she wanted to spend a little more time in Costa Rica with Greg.

"My work here is going to take a little longer than I anticipated." Jenna tried to stay as close to honesty as possible. It was during her afternoon spent exploring the city that Jenna had begun to feel an inner emptiness, as if something was missing from her life. Studying her feelings in depth,

Jenna realized that the experience of being parted from Greg that afternoon had brought up emotions in her that would have otherwise lain dormant. She was missing him: not in the sense that she had spent virtually the last forty-eight hours constantly by his side, and being apart was strange; but a sensation of longing, that was so strong that she was not able nor even willing to fight it. Unconsciously, and eventually consciously, she had chosen to stay longer in Costa Rica than was necessary for her research. She wondered if David would accept her reason for staying on.

"Then, of course, you must stay. I want a thorough job done, Jenna." David was most accommodating. "I'll find some way to delay the Canadian project, so, don't worry. It'll still be there for you when you are finished in Costa Rica."

"Thank you." Jenna tried to sound genuine, but the thought of the Canadian trip hung over her; knowing that she would have to eventually go, spoilt the thoughts she had of staying with Greg for an extra few days.

The line was cracking up, making it difficult for Jenna to hear David.

"I'm sorry to have called you so late," Jenna apologized. It was gone midnight in London. David always worked late, so she was sure she would catch him still in his office. Jenna didn't know if David could still hear her over the rapidly degenerating line. The time was approaching 6.45 and she was due to meet Greg at seven. Hurriedly she ended the telephone call. Her work now taking second place to personal enjoyment, she was eager to hang up and get ready for her evening out with Greg. "I'll phone again. Goodbye, David."

Very faintly she heard him replace the telephone. Jenna put down her own handset, only for the phone to ring again, almost immediately.

"Hello." She was puzzled as to who was calling, as no one, not even David, knew exactly where she was.

"Hi, it's me, Greg." His happiness was evident in the way he spoke.

"How did it go?" Jenna asked, eager to hear how his afternoon had gone at the university.

"Wonderful. It couldn't have been better," Greg enthused. "I'm in the lobby. Will you be down soon?"

"I'll be about ten minutes," Jenna told him. "By the way, I booked seats for a show tonight, curtain goes up at 9.30."

"We'll be there in time," Greg assured her. "I'll meet you in the bar, then we'll go through to the restaurant."

Jenna had brought with her from London the ideal dress to wear on social occasions, due to a lesson learned the previous year. She used to only pack the essentials in a bid to travel light, but when in Italy she had been invited, along with the couple of horse breeders with whom she was staying, to dinner with the Ambassador. Finding herself with nothing suitable to wear, and all chances of purchasing a dress gone as the shops closed, the invite having come with just hours' notice, she had had to borrow an outfit from her hostess. Jenna, a petite size ten, was swamped by a size eighteen evening dress; despite various tactics to disguise the ill-fitting garment with bows and belts, she had still looked a near-comical sight.

As arranged, she meet Greg at the bar, where he had already ordered drinks.

"You look gorgeous." He beamed, looking at her with admiring eyes. "Aren't I the lucky one, to escort such a glamorous lady for a night out on the town?"

Though not one for egotism, Jenna did feel glamorous. A beautiful dress, brushed and styled hair and carefully applied make-up made her feel feminine again. It had been difficult to retain her femininity in the jungle of Monte Verde, with mud caked on her legs, hair unkempt — it proved impossible in the heat and humid atmosphere to keep it in tidy order. It was hopeless wearing make-up, as even the faintest eye shadow or lipstick would have smudged and become unbearably sticky in the tropical forest.

"Then we make an ideal couple," Jenna turned the compliment back on him. "You are very spruce and smart."

Greg laughed, his cheeks flushing slightly with embarrassment. He liked to flatter, but became bashful when complimented himself.

"It's a hired tuxedo," Greg told her, confessing that the clothes weren't his own, as if he was ashamed at the thought that he owned the well-fitting and obviously expensive clothes. "I would never buy one of these. I'd not have anywhere to wear it. Beside that, I couldn't afford it. The cost of rental is the equivalent of buying four shirts."

They went through into the restaurant and were shown to their table in a quiet area, obscured from the rest of the room by discreetly placed pot plants. The sole lighting came from candles.

"What did you do today?" Greg asked her when they were seated.

"Me? We can talk about me later," Jenna chastised him jokingly. "I want to know how you fared at the university. If that broad grin is anything to go by, I'd say you enjoyed yourself."

"Throwing modesty aside, I would say I was a complete success. One hundred per cent. They really took to me." Greg sat back, reliving the afternoon. "It was so rewarding to be asked intelligent questions about my work. We ran on an hour over schedule, just talking. The leatherback turtles proved to be the highlight of my lecture. I was asked by the head of department to arrange an outing for a group of students to the island." He smiled, apologizing. "You don't want to hear all this. I'm rambling on. I'm sorry."

"Don't stop. I want to know." Jenna

reached out, catching hold of one of his hands, an action that seemed natural and instinctive. "I'm interested in you."

Their eyes met. Greg leant across the table, and with his free hand gently brushed her hair back from her cheek. He moved his lips to speak, Jenna's heart beating faster, as her body trembled.

"Are you ready to order, sir?"

The spell had been broken. A few seconds of sheer magic had been lost forever. What had he been going to say? Jenna wondered. When the waiter, left them after taking their order, the conversation turned away from themselves to a mundane topic.

"Is there a fax machine in the village?" Jenna asked him.

"A fax in Tamarindo!" he exclaimed with a laugh. "Yes, sure, along with a dozen computers and a telex."

"I think you're being what is termed as sarcastic." Jenna didn't mind that she was being ridiculed, she had half expected she would be.

"What do you want one for?" Greg wasn't shy about probing.

"I phoned my producer earlier. He was going to send me out the file on my next assignment." She wondered how he would take the news that she was leaving.

"Next assignment, eh?" Greg had become uncomfortable, but was forcing himself to continue talking. "Where?"

"Canada."

"Canada?"

"Yes."

Greg was thoughtful, and Jenna could tell he was turning over in his mind what she had told him.

"When will you be going?"

"After I leave here. I'll be flying straight up."

"And when will that be?" He quickly added, "Don't think I'm trying to get rid of you."

"I don't know when I'll be going." Jenna was truthful.

At this point the waiter returned, bringing their starters. Throughout their dinner they spoke little, each lost in their own thoughts, neither of them far from the subject of her leaving.

The meal finished, they went to the front of the hotel, where the doorman hailed a cab to take them to the theatre. It wasn't until one a.m. that they returned to their hotel. The play they had seen, a contemporary drama, was chiefly aimed at a Costa Rican audience, its dialogue in Spanish. Accustomed to the language, Greg was able to follow the story line, while Jenna, who needed time for a translation into English, managed to grasp the plot but missed the trimmings, as it were.

* * *

"This brings you down to earth with a bump." Greg laughed, as they drove out of the city in his old rickety estate car, leaving behind them a four-star hotel, a night out at the theatre, expensive restaurants and a rented tuxedo. "No more grand living. We're back to normal."

Jenna agreed with him, wondering why he was including her in the 'back to normal'. Their being together was hardly normal.

Neither had been reluctant to leave busy San José, and both were eager to get back to peaceful Tamarindo and Greg's bungalow. Like a weekend cottage in the country, Tamarindo was a quiet retreat from the crowded city.

They drove through dusk into a dark night, exchanging observations on their stay in the city, with both of them lacking the courage to share their deepest thoughts regarding each other. Perhaps it was a fear of rejection on both sides, or maybe a desire to retain the status quo, as if voicing their feelings could, in some way, damage their relationship. There were several times when Greg stopped the car for fuel, or when they slowed to allow an animal to cross the road in front of them, when Jenna wanted to turn and say the things to him that she felt so deeply. At the last moment she lost her nerve and couldn't muster the courage. I'm being foolish, Jenna told herself. Would she be spending her remaining days in Tamarindo with Greg pretending that she thought of him as merely a friend? She truly found her emotions were much stronger, and didn't know how long she could continue hiding them.

"Do you know, I've got so used to not having a TV that I didn't even bother switching on the set in my hotel room," Jenna admitted, surprised at how accustomed she had become to the simple life, and, in her own way, was finding it relaxing.

"It's strange what you can grow used to," Greg said, looking ahead as he concentrated on the road. "I bet you could get accustomed to living here permanently."

"No, never." Jenna spoke before giving what he had said any serious thought. "I'd miss England too much."

"I see," replied Greg, in a response that didn't fit her answer.

Mentally, Jenna kicked herself. Had this been Greg's tentative inquiry as to whether she was prepared, if the occasion should arise, if their relationship did bloom into a romance, there were a lot of 'ifs', to give everything up to live with him in Costa Rica?

If this had been so, Jenna had certainly left him in no doubt whatsoever as to how she felt. The only country in which she wanted to live was England. There would be no changing her mind. She tried to think of a way to backtrack and try not to sound so adamant, but failed to find the words.

Shortly after this exchange they turned into the track that led up to Greg's home, their journey nearly over, with Jenna welcoming the solitude offered by the bungalow. Swinging the car up to the door, Greg switched off the engine and lights.

"I can't see a thing in this darkness,"

Jenna complained with a laugh. "When I first got here you were worried I'd trip over something."

"If you fall over now it'll be your fault, you know where everything is now." The moon half lit Greg's face, revealing his wide, and what Jenna had learnt was slightly mocking, smile.

"What a beautiful sky." Jenna marvelled at the twinkling stars in the heavens above. Turning to look out into the ocean, "What are those lights?"

"Where?" Greg came to her side.

"There. Out on the turtles' island."

In the centre of the island torchlights flickered like a laser show. More swept across the beach. Jenna counted at least four separate beams.

"We've got to get across to the island." There was an urgency in Greg's voice. He took her hand, not with a need to be close to her, but to aid her in the fast descent they were to make to the beach. "Let's get to the boat."

"What is it?" Jenna called, running behind him, fearing she would fall in the almost pitch-black night. "What's wrong?"

"Poachers," was Greg's single-word answer. There was venom in his reply, as if he hated even to say the word. How did he feel about what it described?

Working together in a harmony brought about by the urgency to get across to the turtles' island, Greg and Jenna upturned the rowing boat. One either side, they carried it down to the water's edge. Jenna scrambled aboard, setting the oars up for Greg, who, running through the water, pushed the boat out until it floated. Almost waist-deep in the ocean he grabbed on to the side of the boat and pulled himself in, straight away taking the oars from Jenna. He rowed as if his life depended on it. The oars splashed in and out of the sea, powering the boat through the ocean.

"What do they want with the turtles?"

Jenna spoke quietly, the sea air carrying her voice.

"It's not the turtles they want, but the eggs."

"What for?"

"Big bucks. Those unhatched eggs are worth plenty of dollars."

This was the first time Jenna had seen Greg show any real sign of emotion; he was angry, yet still self-controlled.

"Where can they sell them? Surely as a protected species they wouldn't get anyone to buy the turtles' eggs?"

"They wouldn't be stealing them if they didn't already have a buyer."

Approximately a hundred yards from the shore of the island, Greg stopped rowing and pulled the oars into the boat, allowing the tide to silently carry them into the beach. Making no noise, they pulled the boat up on to the sand, dragging it away from the exposed beach to the shelter of greenery where, barring thorough exploration, it wouldn't be seen.

From the other side of the island

they could hear voices: laughter and shouting, as if the poachers were flaunting their presence.

Greg drew her close and whispered, his lips brushing her ear.

"Hide in the bushes, and no matter what, stay there."

"But Greg . . . " she protested. He put his hand over her mouth to hush her, as, without thinking, she had spoken in an ordinary voice. "I want to come with you."

"It's too dangerous," Greg warned. "They could be armed."

"Armed!" Jenna hadn't realized that poaching was such a serious and violent crime.

"So, get in amid the trees and stay quiet."

Like a frightened animal hiding from its prey, Jenna camouflaged herself in amongst the vines, pulling them across her body in a cries-cross pattern, until she was satisfied she couldn't be seen.

Greg then left, after getting her promise she wouldn't move, an assurance that he probably didn't fully believe she would keep, Jenna considered. When he had told her to stay put in the jungle of Monte Verde, she had wandered off. But now she knew what there was to fear if she did come out of her hiding-place.

In the silence Jenna could hear Greg's footfalls for a while, before an expectant quiet settled in. After a few minutes had passed by, Jenna was aware of a thumping noise, getting louder and louder, faster and faster. It came as a surprise to discover it was her own heartbeat. Jenna tried to calm herself, but the more she thought of the dangerous and possibly violent situation Greg was in, the more she worried.

Should she take the boat back to the mainland for help? A silly thought born out of desperation. She couldn't control the boat alone. Her sole experience of rowing had nearly caused her to drown. Jenna wished that Greg's anger hadn't caused him to act so rashly by coming over to the island with only her accompanying him. He was outnumbered by the poachers at least four to one. Jenna considered she should go after him. In the darkness and confusion of the island, hearing her in the bushes the poachers wouldn't know that she was a girl alone. They might even believe that she was a group of men if she made enough noise. No, Jenna had promised Greg she wouldn't leave her hiding-place. She wasn't going to break another oath.

Hours seemed to have passed. Yet Greg had only been gone five minutes. He should have reached the other side of the island by now, Jenna thought. She was growing uncomfortably hot and cramped, with little room for movement. Insects landed on Jenna, causing her to itch. They crept up her legs and along her arms. Buzzing flies became caught up in her hair; she longed to flick them away.

Raised voices startled her. Panicked shouting reached her ears. Jenna could hear sounds totally alien to the normally peaceful island, heavy thumping and clattering; the place was in turmoil. There was a sharp crack, then silence. Total silence.

There came a crashing through the undergrowth, like a rogue elephant breaking through a jungle. To the right of Jenna, less than ten feet away, were four men. They came running out of the jungle. Even if they had seen Jenna, she was sure they would not have stopped to investigate, such was the state of panic they were in.

They were shouting to each other in Spanish, sounding breathless and terrified, with only one word distinguishable to Jenna.

"*Pistola!*"

Even with her faltering, somewhat classroom based Spanish, Jenna knew what the word meant. "Pistol!"

The jigsaw was piecing together for her. The sharp crack had been a shot from a pistol. Had they fired a warning shot to deter Greg from chasing after them? Or was it worse? Her heart leapt into her mouth. Such had been the anger of Greg, nothing would have stopped him from capturing the poachers. He loved the turtles too much to allow them to be taken from their natural habitat. Jenna couldn't even bring herself to think it, but she had to face the possibility that Greg had been shot.

The men were gone. Jenna could see them speeding across to the mainland in a motorboat, the noisy engine disturbing the island's wildlife.

Jenna came out of her hiding-place. She had to find Greg. They were alone on the island. There was no one she could turn to for help.

"Greg." Jenna shouted for him. Birds shrieked and called as they joined her in her desperate cry. "Greg, where are you? Please, answer me, Greg."

Jenna ran into the jungle, stumbling and falling over as, in her haste, she had little regard for her footing. Scratching her legs and arms, not feeling pain, her whole mind was focused on finding Greg. What would she do if he was hurt, if he was injured, or if, no it was not possible! Surely no one would kill for turtles' eggs? But the eggs were worth a great deal of money, which was a factor that could unbalance the mind of an otherwise non-violent criminal.

With a renewed impetus, she ran deeper into the jungle. It seemed to be taking her ages to reach the beach on the other side of the island. As if experiencing a nightmare, her legs wouldn't move as fast as she wanted, at times almost giving away underneath her.

Suddenly she was on the beach, the soft ground beneath her feet having been replaced by shifting sands.

"Greg!" she called again.

There was no reply. Her feet kicked something. She reached down. It was a torch. Not one that belonged to Greg. It must belong to one of the poachers, Jenna thought, as she switched on the flashlight. The strong yellow beam was thrown out across the beach.

"Oh no!" Jenna gasped, as the light picked out a body lying on the beach. It was Greg. Jenna rushed to his side, falling to her knees.

"Greg. Greg."

She focused the torch's beam on him. His face was pale, and from his brow there came a trickle of blood.

7

"WHAT can I do to help you?" Jenna sat on the sand beside the prone Greg, who was still unconscious. She had wiped the blood from his forehead to find, much to her relief, that though he had been shot, the bullet had only grazed him. "Please, wake up."

There was no response, not even a flickering of his closed eyelids. What could she do to get help? Jenna knew she couldn't leave him, not when he was like this — helpless. Should she light a fire as shipwrecked mariners would? But who would see it? And would anyone come all that distance from the mainland just to investigate what could be an innocent camp fire?

She had to get Greg to the mainland, not vice versa. But how? The only choice was the boat. Jenna couldn't do it. She nearly collapsed in tears at her own inadequacy. Greg might well be seriously injured and she could not get him to where help was. It was this thought, that Greg may be more than just stunned, that drew up Jenna's resolve.

"Don't worry. I'm going to get you to help."

There, she had half achieved it, she had made the decision and told him, now all that was left was to actually carry out her promise. But how could she do that? To be a non-swimmer, stuck on a deserted island, must be one of the biggest handicaps possible. Jenna had the boat. It wasn't a lot, but a start. She could, taking it steady, and applying every caution, row them back to the mainland. Even if she did go off course, it wouldn't matter. If they didn't land at Tamarindo, they could go further up or down the coast. At least then they would be safe. Could she be certain the currents would take them toward Costa Rica? There was a chance the boat could be taken out to sea, to leave them adrift in the middle of the Pacific Ocean. Without food or fresh water they could drift for days, even weeks.

She had to take the gamble. Another problem had to be overcome, which was how was she to get Greg to the boat? Jenna couldn't carry him, she wasn't strong enough. There was no way she could even drag him through the jungle. Walking alone was perilous, and fraught with dangers. She would have to bring the boat to Greg, there was no alternative.

What did the boat weigh? It had to be at least her own weight, probably more. She couldn't carry that. Nor could she drag it through the jungle, first because there was the danger of holing it, second, it was doubtful that it would pass through places where the large trees were no more than two feet apart.

She would have to bring the boat around to the side of the island where

Greg was, by the sea, a thought that filled her with fear. She was prepared to row across to the mainland with Greg on board, but was nervous of bringing the boat around the island alone. She knew Greg would be unable to give any assistance, but at least he would be with her if the current took the boat. If that happened while she was on her own in the boat, Greg would be left on the island with absolutely no chance of help reaching him.

There was one way she could bring the boat round to Greg, like a small tug would bring a giant liner into port. Using the rope that was tied to the bow of the boat for mooring, she could tow it round, paddling through the shallow water close to the shore.

It was a long walk. She was tired and it was dark. The torch would give her light, the desire to help Greg would give her energy and she knew that once she set out on the journey her mind would be concentrated, enabling her to make the journey quickly.

She made sure Greg was comfortable before leaving him. Taking the same route by which she had come, Jenna hurried back to the boat. Each step she took with care. It wouldn't do for both of them to be injured. Jenna hesitated before stepping out from the jungle on to the exposed beach, in case the poachers had come back. She consoled herself that they had been so panicked by their violent action toward Greg that they would possibly never return.

She found that, single-handed, the rowing boat was difficult to move. Once she had extricated it from where they had hidden it, Jenna managed, only by inching it forward a little at a time, to get the boat to the shore-line. Finding a strength that she didn't know she possessed, she pushed the boat into the ocean. Seconds later it was afloat.

Grateful that the sea was warm, not ice-cold like that surrounding Britain at this time of the year, Jenna waded in to where the water came just above her knees. Her legs bare, she was wearing shorts, Jenna kept her shoes on. There was a rough shingle beneath the sand which would have caused her discomfort had she had bare feet.

Once she had moved the boat from inertia, with the rope wrapped firmly around her left hand, the momentum kept it going. She found it was light enough to pull behind her with one hand. In her right hand she held the torch, shining its beam out in front to light her way. She didn't know exactly how long her journey would be. Jenna estimated the trip across the island from beach to beach was approximately a quarter of a mile, so the coastline had to be at least that distance, possibly even more, though the island was very compact, and from the mainland appeared to be rotund.

She was surprised that only half an hour after leaving Greg she was back on the beach where she had left him. Pulling the boat far enough on to the sand to make sure it would not drift away, Jenna began her trip inland.

Greg had gone. Surely it wasn't possible. With such a serious injury he would not have had the strength to stand, and certainly not to walk away. Jenna listened. Was that a motorboat she could hear? Putt-putt-putt. It sounded like an engine in the far distance. Was it possible that the poachers had returned and taken Greg away with them — to hide the evidence of their terrible crime? Or had they returned to silence him — permanently? Jenna found this difficult to believe and hoped she was wrong.

"Greg — Greg!" she called, desperate to find him, guessing that he was unable to answer her. But still she continued to shout. "Greg!"

Jenna stumbled. There was something on the ground, large and heavy. She was nervous to look down, but quickly gained the courage. She sighed a deep breath of relief — it was a tree trunk. Lying along the beach, it must have been there for many years.

It was the wrong beach. No wonder

it had not taken her long to get there. She had come to the wrong beach. And the putt-putt-putt noise? Was she mistaken as to that too? Yes, it wasn't the engine of a boat, but the call of a bird, high above her in the trees.

Jenna ran back to the boat. She had wasted time and energy. Grabbing the rope, she struggled to get it afloat, then it was underway again. Finding the current was beginning to pull at the boat to take it out into the ocean, Jenna tightened her grip and moved in closer to the shore, but far out enough to stop it from bottoming.

How would she recognize the beach Greg was on? He had been closer to the jungle than to the water-line. But the ocean hadn't been that far away, for as Jenna had knelt beside him she had heard the gentle ripple of the sea.

Deciding to sweep the beach with the torch from the sea before bringing the boat up into the sand, she believed the beam would be sure to pick out Greg.

She came round a cluster of rocks

to a small inlet, the beach was a gentle curve of white sand. Using the torch as a searchlight she waved it slowly across the beach, but it revealed nothing. The light began to flutter. In a bid to conserve the energy of the batteries, Jenna switched it off. She would use it only when necessary, finding her way around the shoreline in the light of the moon.

The rope was getting heavy. Several times it had dropped into the ocean and had absorbed water, increasing its weight. Jenna was tired, her arm hurt from pulling the boat. To ease her suffering she decided it was time to pass the rope over to her right hand, to tow the craft the rest of the way with it. Her left hand had become numb with pain, she didn't realize that she had released her grip on the rope. It wasn't until the boat began to drift away from her that she made the discovery. She had lost the craft. The strong current was dragging it away from the shore, three feet from her, four, five, rapidly gaining speed. The boat was her only hope of getting Greg to help, Jenna knew that. She stood, too frightened to go after it, but knowing, for Greg's sake, she must. Another few feet and the boat would be out of her depth.

The decision had to be an instant one. By not going out to the boat she was putting herself before Greg. A previously hidden streak of selfishness tried to convince her that by putting herself in danger she was also risking Greg, for without her he had no one. There was no more time to think, she splashed deeper into the ocean. The water rose to her thighs, then waist-high. She held her arms above her head as the sea rapidly reached her neck-line. A feeling of panic took her, but she couldn't afford to give way to it. The boat was close by, the rope within her reach. The ocean was under her chin, occasionally lapping at her mouth. She sealed her lips for fear of taking in any of the water. Jenna lunged out. Fortune had shone on her. In her first attempt she caught the rope. Turning quickly, she began her semi-walk, semi-swim back to the shore.

As the ocean dropped down to her waist she felt more confident. Retrieving the boat had given a considerable boost to her flagging self-confidence. Breaking into a trot she dragged the boat further in toward the beach.

Suddenly Jenna didn't know what had happened. One moment she was upright, the next she was floundering underwater with the salty sea stinging her eyes. An instinct of self-preservation took over. Scrambling up on to her knees, she got her head above water, then stood. A small indent in the sea floor had caused her to fall. She was thankful for two things, firstly that her tumble hadn't happened in deeper water where she would have found it near-impossible to get to her feet, and secondly that she had had the intelligence to keep a tight grip on the rope, not letting it drift away for a second time.

Soaking wet from head to toe, but fortunately not cold, Jenna carried on toward finding Greg. She tried not to waste a single moment, as every minute was vital.

Less than quarter of an hour later she found Greg. The fading flashlight picked him out, still lying motionless on the sand. The fact Greg hadn't moved worried Jenna, she feared for him. Being unconscious for such a long period could not be regarded as a good sign, but she was relieved to find him in the same spot. Had he come round and wandered off, perhaps back to where they had left the boat, she might have had difficulty in finding him.

Jenna dragged the boat up on to the beach, loosely securing the rope round a nearby tree. She was taking all the precautions that were possible. The boat now was their sole life-line to help.

"Greg." She gently stroked his brow,

hoping that he was now just sleeping, maybe only dazed, and not unconscious. But he seemed to be more comatose than napping. "I'm taking you back to the mainland."

Jenna found talking to him eased the loneliness she was feeling.

"I've got to get you into the boat."

At least now she had solved fifty per cent of her problems. She had Greg and the boat together. No longer were they on opposite sides of the island. Due to her whole body, clothes and hair being wet, the sand she came in contact with stuck to her. Without a mirror she could only imagine that she looked like some type of sand monster.

Should she take Greg to the boat, or the boat to Greg? Which would be easier? The boat to Greg? No, she would then have both the weight of Greg and the boat to pull or push down to the water. She would have to get Greg down to the boat. How could she do that? Jenna was of neither the height nor build to be able to carry him in a 'fireman's lift'. Could she roll him? It seemed a ridiculous idea, almost like a children's game, and he could have internal injuries which she could only exacerbate. Hands under his arms and dragging him was the only, albeit undignified, method she could successfully use.

Trying to evenly distribute the strain through her body, making full use of the cycling-built muscles in her legs, Jenna lifted Greg off the ground. Hurrying to cover as much ground as possible, she was just able to get him half-way down the beach before she needed to take a rest. Under way again, Jenna didn't make another stop until they reached the boat.

"And we thought that was difficult," Jenna mused aloud, as she considered how on earth she was going to get Greg into the boat. The sides of the craft were at least three and a half feet high. She would need to lift Greg four feet off the ground to get him safely into the boat. That wasn't possible. Jenna racked her brain, but she could think of no physical way to actually get Greg into the boat. It was so ironic. If Greg had been conscious, he was practically minded and would have quickly found an answer to her problem. Jenna laughed at the thought, although she didn't feel at all amused.

"Why couldn't you be a seven-stone weakling?" Jenna asked him. "Instead of a big masculine hunk." She brushed back his hair. "And why do I care so much?"

Jenna sat on a small cluster of flat rocks. She felt defeated. She had got so far only to fall at the last fence. Then she had her solution; it was so obvious, she was actually sitting on it. The rocks on which she had sat jutted out over the ocean. It wouldn't be too difficult for her to pull Greg up on to the flat rock that was positioned furthest out. Then with the boat floating underneath, she could gently lower him into it.

It was such an easy arrangement.

Why hadn't she seen it before? A sense of urgency had clouded her thoughts.

"Come on, not much further to go," she told Greg as she dragged him over the lower rocks. "We're nearly there."

Once she reached the large, flat, jutting rock, she lay Greg down, placing him safely away from the edge. If he should regain consciousness there was no risk of him falling. She went back to the boat, untying and pulling it into the sea. Her brief association with the Pacific Ocean had encouraged her to become nautically minded; Jenna knew that she couldn't leave the boat drifting free while she did her best to lower Greg into it, as the current would drag it away. A mooring was necessary. The in-shore current wasn't too fierce, so it didn't need to be very strong. Standing knee-deep in water, beneath the rock on where Greg lay, she looked around for somewhere to attach the rope. No obvious point was forthcoming. Her only option was to jam the rope between two rocks and move quickly, not allowing enough time for it to be wriggled free by the boat's movement.

The rope slipped easily under a small boulder, but it immediately began to work free. Jenna estimated the time she had to get Greg into the boat as probably less than a minute. If Jenna failed in that time, not only would she be back to stage one, but she would have to recover the boat once more.

In went the torch, hitting the floor of the boat accompanied by a glass-shattering sound. Obviously the fall had smashed the lens. Jenna wasn't worried, the batteries had been close to failure, the torch possibly wouldn't have worked again anyway. She manoeuvred Greg into a sitting position, so that his legs dangled over the edge of the rock, his feet touched the boat. Supporting him under the arms she carefully lowered him, making sure that his weight didn't push the boat away.

Greg was safely in the boat, his head at the bow. After getting into the craft herself, Jenna settled Greg comfortably for the trip across to the mainland. Standing, but carefully controlling her balance, she used one of the oars to push the boat away from the rocks and into the mainstream of the current. Sitting down she took up the other oar and started to row.

It didn't take long for Jenna to familiarize herself with the 'mechanics' of the rowing boat. The fact she had to do so out of necessity, seemed to make it easier for her. Jenna found a rhythm in her rowing and, to conserve her energy she rowed slowly, not wanting to tire herself midway across.

Jenna's first course of action was to row round to the other side of the island, where they had landed earlier. The task wasn't very difficult, which gave her confidence, giving her a firm psychological base on which to build for her row across to the mainland.

Turning to look over her shoulder, she could see the lights of mainland Costa Rica. Fortunately, several bonfires were burning fiercely, giving Jenna clear landmarks. There seemed to be some sort of festival or celebration going on in the environs of Tamarindo, for which she was grateful. Without them, her only navigation would have been by luck.

"Agh!" Greg was coming round, though he wasn't yet coherent. "My head!"

He tried to sit up, rocking the boat from side to side as he did so. Jenna feared he would capsize them with his actions.

"Greg, stay still. Don't move." Jenna panicked. She was starting to lose control of the boat.

"What happened?" Greg was confused, the bullet had badly concussed him. Grabbing hold of one side of the boat, he attempted to pull himself into an upright position, but with the swaying of the boat he found it impossible, although he kept trying, causing Jenna to think that the boat was going to turn over. She couldn't allow that to happen. Greg had not yet fully regained consciousness. Were they to turn over, he would be unable to co-ordinate his movements. She hadn't gone to so much trouble to rescue him, only to let him drown now.

"Greg! Don't move!" She had to shout for him to be able to hear her.

Greg slumped back into the bow, his hand to his injured brow.

"Jenna. Where are we?" Gradually he was returning to his normal self, but was very weak. The bullet graze had caused him more harm than she had realized, or possibly it wasn't his only injury.

"We're on our way back."

"How? What? The poachers?" Greg had so many questions to ask. Jenna couldn't answer them all. She needed her concentration to be fixed on her rowing. Greg rubbed his eyes, his vision was blurred and the pitch black of the night didn't help. He suddenly panicked. "Jenna, are you OK?"

"Don't worry. I'm fine." Her reply satisfied him.

Greg calmed, only to become alarmed again seconds later.

"We're in the boat."

"I know." Jenna smiled, amused by his observation.

"Let me take over," he made an attempt at scrambling up on to his knees, grabbing for the oars.

"Sit down." Jenna's barked order startled Greg, who, without questioning her, immediately obeyed. She lowered her voice. "I know you want to take control, but don't worry, I've got everything in hand. You need to rest, that is a nasty wound."

"There's no need to treat me like I'm an invalid." Greg inched along the floor of the boat, to where he knelt beside her.

Jenna pulled the oars into the boat, she knew that she couldn't talk and row competently at the same time. She wasn't taking any risks, and wanted the oars stored safely.

Greg took her hands in his. "I know I have a lot to thank you for. You thought I was unconscious and out of it. And to be truthful, for most of the time I was. But I had these flashes of consciousness, not lasting for more than a second. That was when I found I was being tended by an angel." He leant forward, kissing her gently on the cheek. "I heard you talking, you were comforting me."

"I was reassuring myself," Jenna laughed, embarrassedly. She felt herself becoming awkward and tongue-tied at Greg's attention. She desperately tried to remember. Had she said anything to Greg, that had given away how she felt toward him? In the heat of the moment she had said so much, but she need not worry she told herself, he probably hadn't heard every word she had spoken.

"Jenna . . . " Greg was looking deep into her eyes.

She knew he was about to say something meaningful, to which she would have to respond, and without a carefully thought-out answer, Jenna knew she might be involving herself in a relationship far more complicated than her, or, indeed, his, present lifestyle would permit.

"Could you identify your attackers again?"

Her sudden change of conversation had the desired effect, at the same time, unintentionally upsetting Greg. She could see the hurt in his eyes. Didn't he realize it was for the best? The hurt would be far deeper and more painful if she allowed herself to say what she really felt.

Jenna made a decision. Tomorrow she would organize her return flight to London. She would go to San José. It would be a mistake to spend one day longer in Tamarindo with Greg, for she was becoming too fond of him.

"No, I don't think so. It was very dark, and they were all strangers, I'd never seen any of them before." Greg sat back, prepared now for her to continue rowing the boat. "Luckily I got there before they began to dig up the eggs. So apart from getting myself shot I did manage to achieve something."

"You should be given a medal," Jenna praised him, as she took up the rowing again. "You were very brave."

"No. I was very foolhardy." Greg was critical of himself. "Dashing over to the island with no concern for anything. I should never have allowed you to come along. I shouldn't even have gone myself, it was a job for the authorities, not a self-styled vigilante."

Jenna could see the bonfires of the mainland now on her right. She needed to turn the boat, but the knowledge of how to do so refused to come to her. Jenna was grateful that she was no longer alone in the boat, she had Greg with her in more than just spirit now. She was going to ask him to take over as he had offered. At that time she had not thought him fully capable to handle the vessel. Despite several tries she was unable to turn the boat, and was drifting further down the coast.

"Greg, I think you had better take over."

She got no reply.

"Greg?"

Cloud hid the moon, putting them in complete darkness. Pulling the oars into the boat by sound alone, Jenna reached for the torch, which she could feel bumping against her foot. It made a noise like a baby's rattle, and she was surprised to find that, despite the treatment it had received, the torch worked perfectly, albeit dimly.

Jenna aimed the ray toward Greg's end of the boat. Like a spotlight picking out the star on a dark stage, Greg was captured in the beam. There was no point in her asking him for help, as his earlier consciousness had only been fleeting. He now lay slumped in the bow of the boat, his chin on his chest — out cold.

What am I going to do? Jenna asked herself silently. She had learnt her lesson previously and she wasn't going to talk aloud, despite his appearance, which would have her think he couldn't hear nor understand her. She switched out the light. There was no point in wasting the batteries. Jenna sat in the dark and almost silent night. The only noise to be heard was a gentle rippling of the ocean against the boat as it was carried along.

She was beginning to wonder if she had not made a mistake in trying to get back to the mainland. Maybe it would have been better to have stayed on the island. At least that way she would have been able to tend to Greg's injuries, and afford him all necessary attention. Now adrift in an open boat, like some latter-day Captain Bligh, they were no closer to help.

The island wasn't the Costa Rican equivalent of Piccadilly Circus, but other naturalists like Greg must visit it often, if not daily. She should have left some sign, some mention of what had happened on the island, just in case they didn't reach the mainland as she had planned. That they were drifting in the Pacific Ocean without the prospect of a search party out looking for them, was a frightening thought.

A new enemy was now attacking Jenna — tiredness. She needed to fight to keep her eyes open, the urge to sleep making the lids heavy. Jenna couldn't allow herself to go to sleep, she had to be alert. Not a happy nor experienced sailor, she had no idea of the perils, other than the obvious ones, that lay in the ocean.

She could see, on the clifftop road from Tamarindo, the headlights of a car. How Jenna wished she could exchange places with that untroubled motorist, and how she wished he could see them, being rapidly carried along the coast. But there was no chance. In daylight they were too far away from the mainland to be identifiable, at night it was impossible. There was a chance of being seen if she used the torch as a signalling device for as long as its batteries held out. She had to be careful with what method she used. Jenna wanted to distinguish Greg and herself from ordinary late-night/early-morning fishermen. Greg's small rowing boat wasn't equipped with anything in the way of safety aids, not even a flare. She supposed that he hadn't bothered, as there wasn't a lot that could happen on the relatively short journey from Tamarindo across to the turtles' island.

How could she use the torch in a way to make someone on the mainland realize they were having difficulties? There was a way, and it suddenly dawned on her. A method used and understood internationally — the morse code. She could use the torch to signal an S.O.S. But what was the code for S.O.S.? Jenna couldn't remember. It was always one of the questions used on television shows; she could recall seeing, not that long ago, a general knowledge game show in the States. The correct answer had won the contest, a woman, she recalled, had won $100,000.

S.O.S., the first and last letters had to be the same number of dots or dashes, if only Jenna could remember what it was. She tried to think where she was when she had seen the TV show, anything that would jog her memory. She had been sitting in the lounge bar of a hotel in Boston. Jenna tried to picture herself back there. She had remembered, not the answer from the TV show, but an American sailor had called the morse code across the room shortly before the contestant replied, correctly. Three dots, three dashes, three dots. That was it.

Jenna decided to flash the message to the mainland until either she received a response or the batteries finally died as they were threatening to do. If the former and not the latter happened, she had no need to worry. If the latter occurred, and no help came, Jenna would have to think again. She picked up the torch, pointing it toward the shore. Three long flashes, three brief, then three long. She paused, and waited for a response, none came. Three long, three brief, and three long again.

Jenna saw a light, or had she imagined it? No, there it was again. Several brief flashes, then more, longer ones. She had no idea what the message was, her knowledge of morse code barely covered the basics. In a bid to convey this she repeated the S.O.S.

She was definitely getting a reply. Jenna switched off the torch, and waited, expecting further confirmation that her message had been received, understood and help was on the way. She waited and waited, holding her breath in expectance of seeing the flicker of light on the beach, waiting for a boat to put to sea to come and rescue them. Jenna was looking for the equivalent of a British lifeboat. A small rowing boat like their own would be a welcome sight.

With Greg still unconscious, she longed to hear the comforting voice of another human being, just to reassure her all was well and stop herself feeling so lonely and helpless. She wondered should she signal again? It would probably be pointless. If help was coming it would already be on the way. As the cloud cleared the moon and her eyes reaccustomed themselves to the dark, Jenna could pick out a shape against the shore. The closer it got the clearer it became — it was another boat.

"Greg, we're being rescued!" she cried. A mumble was his only response. He either couldn't understand what she was saying, or more likely, was unable to give an intelligible reply.

Through the water came the whoosh, whoosh, sound of oars. The small rowing boat, now with a beam of light at its bow, was heading straight for them.

"Señorita Fervair!" It was Alberto, and his son was with him, rowing the boat. "*Dondé está Professor Oates?*"

"He's here with me in the boat." Jenna switched on the torch, hoping to illuminate Greg, but the batteries had finally died.

"We been looking many hours for both you." Alberto did his best to speak English, suspecting that Spanish wasn't a language she was strong on. "We catch poacher men. They try steal eggs. We come to island, and no find Professor. He hurt, yes?"

"Yes, he is hurt. We need to get him to doctor."

"Doctor?" Alberto questioned, copying her pronunciation. He apparently didn't know what the word meant.

"We need a *medico* for the professor."

Alberto indicated that he understood. The two boats touched, giving Alberto the opportunity to pull the rope from Greg and Jenna's boat into his own. He tied the rope to the rear of his boat. Obviously, like a broken-down car, they were to be towed back to Tamarindo.

I'm going home tomorrow, Jenna thought as the boat rippled through the water. She would go directly to

London, and not up to Canada as her producer had suggested. Jenna needed time to be alone, and rebuild the emotional wall that the handsome and caring Professor Oates had, brick by brick, pulled down. She would be leaving behind both a paradise and a Prince Charming.

The boats came into shallow water by the shore. Alberto leapt out and pulled Greg and Jenna's boat on to the beach. Jenna was so relieved to be back on the mainland that she could have cried, but there was no time for that. Though she felt like collapsing on to the sand, they had to get Greg to a doctor, quickly.

8

"I ONCE had a teddy bear that looked like you do now." Jenna tried to cheer Greg, as he came from the doctor's surgery into the makeshift waiting room where she was sitting. Wrapped around his head, keeping a large square pad of cotton wool in place, was a clean, white bandage.

"I hope he felt better than I do." Greg was in good humour, showing no self-pity.

"I think he was probably worse — his ear had fallen off."

"At least I'm not suffering from anything so serious."

"What did the doctor say?" Jenna walked beside Greg out of the house where the surgery was based and to Alberto's pick-up.

"He said I was lucky only to have

been grazed. If the bullet had gone a little to the left," Greg threw his hands into the air, shrugging his shoulders, "who knows whether I'd be here now."

"But you are, that's all that counts." Jenna slipped an arm around his waist, giving him a brief hug.

"Only because of you." He put his finger under her chin, raising it so that their eyes met. "You saved my life, Jenna. Without you I could still be out there."

"I'm returning the favour." She felt embarrassed by his gratitude and tried to brush it off. "I still owe you one. You rescued me twice."

"I hope I never have to call on you again, so that we can be equal." Greg smiled. His lips moved to form a word, then changed to another smile.

He wanted to say something else, Jenna could sense it. Something that could, if she wasn't careful, destroy her resolve to begin her journey back to London today.

"I'm dead on my feet." Jenna filled

the gap caused by his hesitancy. "I need to sleep."

She considered telling him that she was going home, but decided that she had better impart that piece of information when they were alone, and not with Alberto, who sat waiting impatiently in the driver's seat of his truck, present.

"*Cómo está Ud?*" Alberto asked Greg, as he opened the passenger door of the truck for him.

"I'm on the mend, thank you, Alberto." Greg restricted the conversation to English, not wanting Jenna to feel left out.

He refused the offer to sit in the cab, joining Jenna in the rear of the pick-up.

"I guess this means the documentary is definitely off. I can't imagine your company wanting to film me after I nearly had their researcher killed."

"I think you may have sealed your own fate, there."

"I have?" Greg was disappointed at

the thought of no documentary.

"Yes. I'm sure now they won't be able to resist you."

"Really? Wonderful." Greg was genuinely pleased.

"I think they'll find your story too interesting to ignore."

"When will you get an answer for certain?"

"I should see David tomorrow. Then I will write to you and confirm the answer."

"Slow down one minute. What do you mean 'see David tomorrow'? I'm sure he's not coming out here." Greg was puzzled. "Are you going home?"

"Yes."

"That's rather sudden. I thought you had no need to rush away."

"I don't. Well, I don't and I do." Jenna became flustered.

"Which is it?" Greg could tell she was keeping something back.

"As much as I like being here, I have a job to do. I can't stay for a holiday, which I am doing, and there's no more I have to do for my work." Jenna was honest with him, but omitted the real reason why she was leaving so suddenly — that she was falling in love with him.

"You'll let me drive you into San José, won't you?" Greg was insistent that she did.

"Of course. I would appreciate it if you did."

They didn't speak again until Alberto left them outside of Greg's bungalow.

"What time does your flight leave?"

"I don't know, if I have to wait I'll book in at a hotel."

"Why not phone from the village and get an exact time?" Greg was puzzled by what seemed her desire to leave Tamarindo as soon as she could. "That way you could stay on here, and drive up a few hours before the plane was due to take off. Then you wouldn't have to kill time in San José."

"I'd prefer it this way." Jenna realized too late that she had sounded ungrateful, in response to his kind offer.

"Right." Greg didn't want to make any more suggestions, probably fearing he would have them thrown back in his face.

* * *

"Are you sure you don't want to telephone from the village?" Greg asked again as they sat eating their breakfast, a meal they were consuming at noon due to the previous night's events causing them to sleep on until mid-morning.

"I'll go straight to San José. If I have time to spare I can begin my report on your work for my producer."

It was crazy. Jenna was treating Greg as if he were a stranger, yet the reason for returning home sooner than she would like to was because she was becoming too attached to him.

"I'll miss not having you around," Greg admitted. "Life will be very boring. Do you think you will come back with the film crew?"

"No. I won't be needed. I'll probably

be on the other side of the world by that time." She laughed.

Thinking constantly of you and wishing I was with you, Jenna confessed to herself, wondering if the pain she felt at the thought of parting from him would increase or decrease when she actually left him at the airport, and her aeroplane took off.

Two old and opposing clichés ran through her mind: 'out of sight, out of mind' and 'absence makes the heart grow fonder'. Jenna wondered which was the truer; knowing that soon she would discover for herself.

"A penny for them."

"Pardon?"

"A penny for your thoughts."

Jenna hadn't realized that her preoccupation with the next few hours had turned her into poor company.

"Sorry, I didn't realize I was miles away. I should mind my manners," Jenna apologized.

"I hope I've not become so boring that you have to escape from me in your thoughts," Greg joked, leaving her the opportunity to tell him what was occupying her.

"No, of course not," Jenna answered truthfully, then added a little white lie. "I'm about to return to the real world, I have to make plans."

"Then you don't consider that here, where I live, is a real world?" Greg made it awkward for her to answer, she had either to offend him or lie.

"It's not a real world to most people." She gave a non-committal reply, sitting firmly on the fence. "Were it so, then we would not be even considering making a documentary of your work."

Jenna was pleased with herself, throughout breakfast she had been able to keep him at a verbal arm's length.

"I'll help with the washing up," Jenna suggested as they cleared away the crockery.

"No need." Greg left the cups and plates in the kitchen sink. "I'll do it when I get home."

Home alone, Jenna thought, wishing that she would be returning from San José with him. It was her own fault. If she wanted, Jenna could spend the rest of the day, the rest of the week, or month, year, even the rest of her life with Greg Oates. She could admit her feelings to him, and ignore the consequences of having to leave her job, her family, her home in England, to live with the man she loved in Costa Rica. Did she truly love him so as to give everything up for him? She had no doubts — yes, she did.

Then why didn't she? It was a question Jenna asked herself, and had been asking for the last twenty-four hours. She knew the answer, and was frightened that what she feared would be true that Greg didn't feel love of the same intensity for her as she did for him. She had no doubt that a feeling much deeper than friendship flowed between them; Greg had evidenced in his actions that he was attracted to her. But Jenna felt she needed a further, more substantial show of commitment, before she would risk showing her cards, as it were.

Though it was not a serious worry, Jenna wondered if she could trust her emotions. Now, while she was here in Tamarindo with Greg, it was easy to think she was in love with him. But back in London, with thousands of miles separating them, would she still feel so strongly? When she couldn't see his caring smile and the cheeky twinkle in his eyes and had to rely on memory to bring them back to her, would she be longing to be with him?

The answer had to be yes, a resounding and most definite yes. Jenna was an intelligent woman, mature beyond her years, a quick thinker who made fast decisions that she always stuck to. When flat-hunting she knew the type of apartment she wanted, viewed it once, then exchanged contracts just days later, and had lived happily in her new home ever since, at no time regretting her decision.

Jenna felt just as sure in this situation, but was that enough? Both she and Greg needed to make a commitment to each other. When would they ever get to that stage in their relationship? Jenna had not even consciously hinted to him of her love. A lot had to change between them over the next few hours for her to freely admit her feeling without fear of being hurt by an unfavourable response from him.

Jenna knew she had to tell him. If she didn't, she knew it would be an omission she would always regret. Yet if she did speak up it could cause her a lot of heartache.

"Are you all packed?" Greg asked as he came out of the kitchen, ready to leave.

"I was first thing this morning." Jenna replied. "I don't take long, not a lot to pack."

"Shall we go?" Greg opened the front door of the bungalow, taking his favourite hat off the peg behind the door, and putting it on his head, covering the bandage that made him look like a refugee from Custer's Last Stand.

I could also make an absolute idiot of myself, Jenna thought, he probably hasn't the faintest idea of how I feel. Such a bolt from the blue could make him regard her as foolish. What if that did happen? Greg might treat it as a joke, probably even telling the film crew when they arrived, making her a laughing stock among her colleagues.

No, one thing that Greg wasn't was insensitive. Jenna was being silly in thinking that he would find her feelings amusing. They got into the car, with Greg roaring the engine into life, and Jenna remembered her first sighting of Greg, or more accurately of his car. She had thought it was a taxi. Later she learnt that the cabs of San José were of a far superior standard to Greg's transport.

The turtles' island looked peaceful, as Jenna took her final view of it as they drove away from Greg's bungalow.

Its colourful flora wouldn't reproduce exactly on film, and she felt a little sorry for future viewers of the documentary who would be unable to see the vivid crimsons, sparkling yellows and host of other brilliant colours that covered the island. Neither would they be able to smell the sweet scents that drifted from the many and varied plants through the humid air of rural Tamarindo.

Throughout their journey, Greg was eager to talk, and rarely was there a lull in the conversation. Jenna had the impression that Greg was treating her leaving lightly. As if she was a relative who had stayed for the weekend and was now taking the train home, which was maybe no more than a hundred miles away. Instead of her being — she couldn't think of what term she could use to describe their relationship — instead of being a friend who was flying thousands of miles across the world, and whom he would probably never see again.

Jenna couldn't bear that thought.

She tried to push it from her mind, but it kept creeping back, niggling at her. Once she took her first step on to the aeroplane she wouldn't be able to go back, she would be at the point of no return.

You know I don't want to leave, because I love you. That's what Jenna wanted to say, just a few words which would mean a lot and end the uncertainty she felt.

San José wasn't that far ahead, as they drove past the small, ramshackle café where they had eaten on the day of Jenna's arrival. Then it had meant nothing, now there was a special place for it in Jenna's heart. It was neither a romantic setting nor in anyway picturesque, but Jenna blocked its negative points from her mind, only remembering it as the place where they had taken their first meal together.

"They arrested the poachers," Greg told her as they entered the city. "Alberto came to the house before you were awake this morning."

"Good." Jenna tried to put spirit into her answer, but could find no emotion to spare. It was as if her whole being was concentrated on her feelings toward Greg.

"We should have stopped for a coffee," Greg looked at his watch. "It's nearly six. I doubt there's a flight this evening. You could have telephoned from the café and checked."

"No. I'll go straight to the airport, and find out there." What Jenna wanted to say was — I don't want to delay leaving for any longer than I have to. Every minute more I spend with you makes me want to stay.

"OK. The airport it is."

Ahead of them the traffic was slowly coming to a halt due to an accident that blocked the street. Greg swung the car into a side road, hoping to avoid the blockage by means of a detour. Unfortunately despite taking several turnings, it brought them back to the street they had tried to avoid, with the accident still ahead of them.

"I can walk from here." Jenna knew from her memory of the day she had spent alone in the city, that the airport was a couple of blocks to the north of them. She would be able to walk the distance in under ten minutes. "It's not far."

"Do you think my driving is dangerous?" Greg asked, his question very direct.

"No. Why?" Jenna wondered what she had done or said to make him ask such a thing.

"Then why are you so eager to get away?"

"I thought I'd save you the drive to the airport." Jenna knew she hadn't spoken the truth. "You've no need to wait in this queue, you can turn and head out of the city."

"I want to make sure there is a flight for you," Greg was honest with her. "I don't want to leave you stranded at the airport."

There was no 'I don't want you to go' from Greg. His priority was that Jenna catch her plane.

The traffic began to move past the accident, an overturned cart which had now been moved to one side, allowing cars to pass.

"We're moving again now," Greg told her. "So you may as well travel in comfort."

There were no more delays, and minutes later, Greg pulled the car up outside the airport terminal building. Jenna reached into the rear of the vehicle to retrieve her luggage. Greg put his hand on her arm.

"Come back for it if there's a flight," he suggested. "It'll save you dragging it around the airport. And if not I'll drive . . . "

Jenna interrupted him. "Drive me to a hotel."

"Yes, if you insist." Greg would have preferred that she return to Tamarindo with him, and come back to San José in time for her flight.

Getting out of the car, hopefully for the last time, Jenna went into the building, with the wish that not only was a flight soon to leave but there would also be a free seat.

"There's a flight to London leaving at twenty hundred hours," Jenna was told. "And yes, there are seats available."

With less than an hour to wait, and most of that would be occupied with airport officialdom, Jenna would find the time passing quickly, and she wouldn't have the opportunity to dwell on her feelings for Greg, and what would certainly be her regrets.

"It's a good job we didn't have that coffee, you would have missed your flight," Greg said as he pulled her suitcase from the back seat and handed it to Jenna. They stood side by side on the pavement by his car.

There was an awkwardness between them, neither knowing how to say goodbye. Did they shake hands or kiss? They eventually settled for a peck on the cheek.

"If you are ever in London," Jenna made a polite invitation that he should call on her.

"Thank you." Greg bit his lip, at a loss for words. Then he looked at his watch. "You had better hurry along, I don't want to be the cause of you missing your flight."

"Goodbye, then." Jenna found it difficult to speak.

"Have a good journey." Greg got back into his car, starting the engine, the familiar fierce rumble of the motor a reminder to Jenna of the times they had shared.

Jenna stood on the kerb's edge watching as he drove away. Don't go, I love you, her heart shouted as Greg disappeared from view. He was gone. Jenna turned into the building, regretting that she hadn't told him how she felt; at the same time grateful that she had not spoken out. Greg had also had the opportunity to confess his emotional bond to her, which he hadn't: proving to Jenna that her love for him was an emotional one-way street.

"Will you be paying by cash or credit card?"

"I'm sorry, what was that?" Jenna hadn't been concentrating on what the girl on the ticket desk was saying.

"Cash or credit card?"

"Card." Jenna's mind suddenly snapped into gear. "No, forget it. I don't want the ticket. I'm not catching the flight."

"I'm sorry, madam, I thought you . . . " The assistant was confused. "I thought you wanted a flight to London?"

"I did. But I don't now." Picking up her suitcase Jenna ran from the desk. She had something to do, something she should have done before now.

More sure now than she had ever been in her life, Jenna hurried out to the airport's taxi rank, speaking to the driver of the cab at the head of the rank.

"*Es Ud se elquila?*" Jenna asked if his taxi was for hire in uncertain Spanish.

"Yes."

Jenna was fortunate to find a driver who spoke English. She got into the rear of the car.

"Would you drive out on the Quepos road, I want to stop a car."

"You police lady. This cops and robbers, yes?" The driver became enthusiastic. Starting the engine he pulled away at speed, under the illusion that he was aiding the capture of criminals.

Jenna didn't know how far ahead of them he was, but even if she had to take the taxi all the way to Tamarindo she was going to find him — and tell Greg she loved him. She hoped he may have stopped at the café outside the city, and she would have no difficulty in finding him there.

The taxi-driver's knowledge of San José's streets exceeded that of Greg, and shortly after leaving the centre of the city they were nearing its outskirts.

Jenna's heart was beating fast, so eager was she to find Greg.

"What this criminal done?" The taxi-driver's English language was good, but his grammar needed work.

Jenna wasn't prepared to go into a lengthy explanation for the cabbie, or burst his bubble of fantasy that had him believe he was chasing a getaway car.

"He's stolen my heart."

"Then we get it back for you," the driver said, evidencing that his bi-lingual capabilities weren't so good as Jenna had first thought.

"Quickly, turn around." Jenna shouted to the driver, who immediately swung the taxi across two lanes of busy traffic, incurring the wrath of many road-users.

Jenna had seen Greg's car. He was driving towards San José, a determined look on his face, his hands gripping the steering-wheel tightly.

Where could he be going, Jenna wondered, and at such a fast speed? The taxi-driver had great difficulty in catching him. Greg's car was old and rusty, but certainly not cumbersome.

"*Delanteros faros*." Jenna was trying to get the cabbie to flash his headlights to attract Greg's attention, but didn't know how to ask him; she had to keep repeating the Spanish for headlights until he understood.

The indicator of Greg's car came on and he pulled the vehicle into the side of the road; the Costa Rican taxi-driver stopped the cab behind it.

Jenna leapt from the rear of the taxi, running to where Greg was getting out of the driver's side, a startled look on his face.

"Jenna! What are you doing here? You should be at the airport." Greg spoke in a rush.

"I couldn't go."

"I'm so glad." Greg caught hold of her hands.

"I don't want to leave you, Greg." The words flowed from Jenna's lips. "I love you."

"And I love you, that's why I was coming back, to tell you." Greg spoke with sincerity. "I've been offered a post at London University, and once the documentary has been filmed I intend to take it up. Before that I want to marry you, Jenna. Will you be my wife?"

"Yes." All Jenna's dreams were coming true. "What about your beloved Costa Rica?"

"I told you that I'd never got over being homesick," Greg smiled as he took her into his arms.

THE END

Other titles in the Linford Romance Library:

A YOUNG MAN'S FANCY
Nancy Bell

Six people get together for reasons of their own, and the result is one of misunderstanding, suspicion and mounting tension.

THE WISDOM OF LOVE
Janey Blair

Barbie meets Louis and receives flattering proposals, but her reawakened affection for Jonah develops into an overwhelming passion.

MIRAGE IN THE MOONLIGHT
Mandy Brown

En route to an island to be secretary to a multi-millionaire, Heather's stubborn loyalty to her former flatmate plunges her into a grim hazard.

WITH SOMEBODY ELSE
Theresa Charles

Rosamond sets off for Cornwall with Hugo to meet his family, blissfully unaware of the shocks in store for her.

A SUMMER FOR STRANGERS
Claire Hamilton

Because she had lost her job, her flat and she had no money, Tabitha agreed to pose as Adam's future wife although she believed the scheme to be deceitful and cruel.

VILLA OF SINGING WATER
Angela Petron

The disquieting incidents that occurred at the Vatican and the Colosseum did not trouble Jan at first, but then they became increasingly unpleasant and alarming.

DOCTOR NAPIER'S NURSE
Pauline Ash

When cousins Midge and Derry are entered as probationer nurses on the same day but at different hospitals they agree to exchange identities.

A GIRL LIKE JULIE
Louise Ellis

Caroline absolutely adored Hugh Barrington, but then Julie Crane came into their lives. Julie was the kind of girl who attracts men without even trying.

COUNTRY DOCTOR
Paula Lindsay

When Evan Richmond bought a practice in a remote country village he did not realise that a casual encounter would lead to the loss of his heart.

ENCORE
Helga Moray

Craig and Janet realise that their true happiness lies with each other, but it is only under traumatic circumstances that they can be reunited.

NICOLETTE
Ivy Preston

When Grant Alston came back into her life, Nicolette was faced with a dilemma. Should she follow the path of duty or the path of love?

THE GOLDEN PUMA
Margaret Way

Catherine's time was spent looking after her father's Queensland farm. But what life was there without David, who wasn't interested in her?

HOSPITAL BY THE LAKE
Anne Durham

Nurse Marguerite Ingleby was always ready to become personally involved with her patients, to the despair of Brian Field, the Senior Surgical Registrar, who loved her.

VALLEY OF CONFLICT
David Farrell

Isolated in a hostel in the French Alps, Ann Russell sees her fiancé being seduced by a young girl. Then comes the avalanche that imperils their lives.

NURSE'S CHOICE
Peggy Gaddis

A proposal of marriage from the incredibly handsome and wealthy Reagan was enough to upset any girl — and Brooke Martin was no exception.

A DANGEROUS MAN
Anne Goring

Photographer Polly Burton was on safari in Mombasa when she met enigmatic Leon Hammond. But unpredictability was the name of the game where Leon was concerned.

PRECIOUS INHERITANCE
Joan Moules

Karen's new life working for an authoress took her from Sussex to a foreign airstrip and a kidnapping; to a real life adventure as gripping as any in the books she typed.

VISION OF LOVE
Grace Richmond

When Kathy takes over the rundown country kennels she finds Alec Stinton, a local vet, very helpful. But their friendship arouses bitter jealousy and a tragedy seems inevitable.

CRUSADING NURSE
Jane Converse

It was handsome Dr. Corbett who opened Nurse Susan Leighton's eyes and who set her off on a lonely crusade against some powerful enemies and a shattering struggle against the man she loved.

WILD ENCHANTMENT
Christina Green

Rowan's agreeable new boss had a dream of creating a famous perfume using her precious Silverstar, but Rowan's plans were very different.

DESERT ROMANCE
Irene Ord

Sally agrees to take her sister Pam's place as La Chartreuse the dancer, but she finds out there is more to it than dyeing her hair red and looking like her sister.

HEART OF ICE
Marie Sidney

How was January to know that not only would the warmth of the Swiss people thaw out her frozen heart, but that she too would play her part in helping someone to live again?

LUCKY IN LOVE
Margaret Wood

Companion-secretary to wealthy gambler Laura Duxford, who lived in Monaco, seemed to Melanie a fabulous job. Especially as Melanie had already lost her heart to Laura's son, Julian.

NURSE TO PRINCESS JASMINE
Lilian Woodward

Nick's surgeon brother, Tom, performs an operation on an Arabian princess, and she invites Tom, Nick and his fiancé to Omander, where a web of deceit and intrigue closes about them.

THE WAYWARD HEART
Eileen Barry

Disaster-prone Katherine's nickname was "Kate Calamity", but her boss went too far with an outrageous proposal, which because of her latest disaster, she could not refuse.

FOUR WEEKS IN WINTER
Jane Donnelly

Tessa wasn't looking forward to meeting Paul Mellor again — she had made a fool of herself over him once before. But was Orme Jared's solution to her problem likely to be the right one?

SURGERY BY THE SEA
Sheila Douglas

Medical student Meg hadn't really wanted to go and work with a G.P. on the Welsh coast although the job had its compensations. But Owen Roberts was certainly not one of them!

HEAVEN IS HIGH
Anne Hampson

The new heir to the Manor of Marbeck had been found. But it was rather unfortunate that when he arrived unexpectedly he found an uninvited guest, complete with stetson and high boots.

LOVE WILL COME
Sarah Devon

June Baker's boss was not really her idea of her ideal man, but when she went from third typist to boss's secretary overnight she began to change her mind.

ESCAPE TO ROMANCE
Kay Winchester

Oliver and Jean first met on Swale Island. They were both trying to begin their lives afresh, but neither had bargained for complications from the past.

CASTLE IN THE SUN
Cora Mayne

Emma's invalid sister, Kym, needed a warm climate, and Emma jumped at the chance of a job on a Mediterranean island. But Emma soon finds that intrigues and hazards lurk on the sunlit isle.

BEWARE OF LOVE
Kay Winchester

Carol Brampton resumes her nursing career when her family is killed in a car accident. With Dr. Patrick Farrell she begins to pick up the pieces of her life, but is bitterly hurt when insinuations are made about her to Patrick.

DARLING REBEL
Sarah Devon

When Jason Farradale's secretary met with an accident, her glamorous stand-in was quite unable to deal with one problem in particular.

THE PRICE OF PARADISE
Jane Arbor

It was a shock to Fern to meet her estranged husband on an island in the middle of the Indian Ocean, but to discover that her father had engineered it puzzled Fern. What did he hope to achieve?

DOCTOR IN PLASTER
Lisa Cooper

When Dr. Scott Sutcliffe is injured, Nurse Caroline Hurst has to cope with a very demanding private case. But when she realises her exasperating patient has stolen her heart, how can Caroline possibly stay?

A TOUCH OF HONEY
Lucy Gillen

Before she took the job as secretary to author Robert Dean, Cadie had heard how charming he was, but that wasn't her first impression at all.